JAYA GANGA

Vijay Singh is an Indian novelist, screenplay-writer and filmmaker living in Paris.

After studying history at St Stephen's College, Delhi, and the Centre for Historical Studies, Jawaharlal Nehru University, Delhi, he moved to Ecole des Hautes Etudes en Sciences Sociales, Paris, for his doctoral work.

Since the early eighties, he has written extensively for Le Monde, Le Monde Diplomatique, Libération, The Guardian and other international and Indian newspapers.

Vijay Singh is the author of several internationally-acclaimed books, including Jaya Ganga, In Search of the River Goddess, La Nuit Poignardée, Whirlpool of Shadows and The River Goddess. In a selection made by the Booker Prize-winner Barry Unsworth, Whirlpool of Shadows was listed in the Sunday Times (UK) as a 'Best Book of 1992'. His books have been translated into French and other European languages.

Over the last two decades, he has written and directed five acclaimed films which have been showcased at scores of international film festivals, often in competition. He is currently working on several projects, including his next feature, The Palace Symphony, which is adapted from his novel Whirlpool of Shadows.

Praise for the book

A journey that teaches you to swim through the enigmas of this world.
—Jean-Claude Carrière (Oscar-winner) in *Liberation*

Almost a new style of writing is born: less cerebral and convoluted than Rushdie, less formal than Anita Desai, less clever than Vikram Seth but certainly more wholesome and fulfilling for the modern Indian soul.
—Aman Nath in *The Times of India*

If you want something labeled travel, pick quality spiced stuff, like *Jaya Ganga*.
—*The Guardian* (London)

Poetic, mystical, metaphysical, humorous, erotic, erratic, this book is a complete portrait of India.
—Yves Florenne in *Le Monde Diplomatique*

Beyond the present, this journey is a pilgrimage to the very source of religion, art and history. It is a meditation on time and the tragedy of existence... Jaya Ganga, whose baroque effervescence at times brings Umberto Eco to mind, is not just one of the most original books of recent times, it also heralds the birth of a writer.
—Michelle Perrot in *Le Nouvel Observateur*

This novel is the very air that India breathes. Its great quality is to inspire thought.
—Antoine Spire in *Le Matin*

Jaya Ganga is a literary event, the revelation of an immense talent.
—J.B. in *La Montagne*

A shocking adventure—mystical, romantic, erotic. The Ganga is that huge boulevard where sages and prostitutes share a common destiny...
—Jean-Paul Ribes in *Actuel*

JAYA GANGA

Vijay Singh

RUPA

Revised edition published by
Rupa Publications India Pvt. Ltd 2021
7/16, Ansari Road, Daryaganj
New Delhi 110002

Sales centres:
Allahabad Bengaluru Chennai
Hyderabad Jaipur Kathmandu
Kolkata Mumbai

Copyright © Vijay Singh 1985, 1989, 1990, 2006, 2021

PAP
TAGORE

The edition is published with the support of the Publication Assistance
Programmes of the Institut Français

First published in French by Editions Ramsay, Paris 1985
First English edition published by Penguin Books 1989 (India), 1990 (UK)
New edition published by Rupa Publications India 2006

This is a work of fiction. Names, characters, places and incidents are
either the product of the author's imagination or are used
fictitiously and any resemblance to any actual person, living or
dead, events or locales is entirely coincidental.

All rights reserved.
No part of this publication may be reproduced, transmitted,
or stored in a retrieval system, in any form or by any means,
electronic, mechanical, photocopying, recording or otherwise,
without the prior permission of the publisher.

ISBN: 978-93-5520-003-7

First impression 2021

10 9 8 7 6 5 4 3 2 1

The moral right of the authors has been asserted.

Printed by Thomson Press India Ltd., Faridabad

This book is sold subject to the condition that it shall not,
by way of trade or otherwise, be lent, resold, hired out, or otherwise
circulated, without the publisher's prior consent, in any form of binding or
cover other than that in which it is published.

for my mother
for my father
Raksha and Hari
two waves of the Ganga today

Works By The Same Author

BOOKS

La Nuit Poignardée, les Sikhs, Flammarion, Paris, (1987)

Jaya Ganga, In Search of the River Goddess, Penguin Books, London, (1990)

Whirlpool of Shadows, Jonathan Cape, London, (1992)

The River Goddess, Gallimard Jeunesse, Moonlight, London, (1994)

Ballerina, co-author, Escales d'auteurs, Editions du Palais, Paris, (2000)

In Search of the Sacred Sin, with Gabriella Wright, in Nouvelles du Cinéma, Seuil, Paris, (2004)

Ganga, co-author, Oxford University Press, Delhi, (2014)

Gange, Fleuve de déesse, Editions de la Flandonnière, Paris, (2014)

FILMS WRITTEN AND DIRECTED BY VIJAY SINGH

Man and Elephant (1989)

Jaya Ganga (1996)

One Dollar Curry (2004)

Bhopali (screenplay, co-author, 2004)

India by Song, 2010

Farewell My Indian Soldier, (2015)

The Palace Symphony (in development)

Ode

THERE IS A LITTLE SKETCH ON THE DOOR OF MY STUDIO. It is in charcoal. It is raw. It is fragile. It lives for it can never die. A woman had sat up all night making it. The morning after, she left behind her reproach–the image of a woman leaving the threshold of a house. It is often the women you have loved the least who leave behind the final judgement on your life. Leaving, she whispered, women shall always exit the doors of your life. She had summed it all up in one single phrase of truth that children alone are capable of.

It was an autumn night. The first rays of cold entered obliquely through the window, like shafts of translucent light. The rusted kerosene lamp burnt, its quivering crimson flame as lonesome as the sketch on the parched door. I was restless, gripped by a sacred insomnia. I had erred in life. Like Othello, I had to pay homage to the gods.

I walked out of the studio to melt into the night. The slight curve on *Rue Hallé* below resembled a sudden twist in a very personal destiny. A car screeched, stopped, turned and whizzed past to inform me that I was drunk. No, my holy witness, we are never drunk, it is the times that are drunk. Alcohol only reveals that we are but cogs in the larger wheel of time.

Avenue René Coty is the only road that leads to the absolute. Its end in Parc Montsouris announces the silent end of a life and the beginning of another. A unique mental track, it is on this road that each season leaves behind its final autograph.

I walked down the Avenue. The autumn before me was melting dark brown, wide awake to the secret of a farewell night. The gates to Parc Montsouris were shut. *No entry after 8 p.m.*, they announced in red and white. The municipality of Paris wanted to impose on me its sense of criminal security. I jumped over the gates to step into the pitch dark of a garden whose darkness was rendered transparent by the spirits of a bygone necropolis. At the feet of the Moroccan observatory, there was a flower bed which had all the species and colours of flowers offered to this earth. I had no reason to love flowers, I had never loved them, I had never offered them, but I had to pay homage to the gods, my gods who knew no churches or temples or mosques.

I plucked four chrysanthemums, five roses, five marigolds and eleven jasmines. In all, twenty-five flowers, for the number of years she had been on this planet. To lend the flowers the shape of union, I plucked a branch of *raat ki raani*, the queen of night, the creeper-flower which alone can sum up the destiny of the most indefinable night. Together, I strung them all with a holy white thread, the thread with which my mother had celebrated my birth on this planet of eternal riddles.

I walked all night, lost in the haze of a Parisian drizzle. After several hours, I reached the long-awaited waters. The water was opaque. It flowed silently, breathing like a woman after the storm of love was over.

I lit some incense. The black paste produced a viscous white smoke that flattened out over the sheet of water. The air smelt of ceremony, the wind played flute. In the pin-drop quiet of a Parisian night, I cracked a coconut on a cobble-stone to allow her spirit to escape the mundane trappings of this earth. The coconut and the garland, the vermilion and the *kohl*, the glass bangles and the *parandah*, all that was her love and her promise,

I offered them to the Seine with the firm belief that all rivers lead to Ganga.

Jaya had left twelve hours ago. Before she left, I had applied *sindhoor*, a bright red streak of vermilion, along the parting of her hair. Completing the act of Hindu heresy, allowing herself the gamble of another marriage, she had graced my hair, too, with a thin line of the same colour. The rite was done. *Sindhoor* means union, and union is the seed of disunion. *Sindhoor* is tragedy, for tragedy is nothing but the first union.

We parted just when we had desired each other the most. We met and separated as the innocent children of a magical 'objective chance', to which alone we had ever offered our pagan salutations. Two beings brought together by an external causality, two beings severed by an external causality, this is the only moment when love resembles history and history, love. We are the children of a capricious history, and history is the mysterious teardrop of our Pierrot-child…

Jaya flew away to her nuptial home and I took the airport coach back to Paris.

The sun, a misty orange ball, was rolling out of the frizzy hair of an Algerian girl seated beside me. Its rays illuminated a whole universe and yet nothing existed in my empire of an absolute absence. Deep inside me, I saw Jaya, wearing a light grey *pashmeena* shawl, soaked wet in the colours of a Gangetic sunset. I felt the fragrance of her breath rise slowly towards the night. I saw her feet dangle gently above the rippling surface of Ganga. I touched her thigh, and Ganga smiled.

Absence does not mean sorrow. Pleasure and sadness are too mundane to wear the crown of cosmic states of mind. An absolute absence captures completely, if fugitively, an absolute presence. Absence illuminates the inner world as a tiny fire-fly lights up the most impregnable night. Jaya was a fire-fly lit before the eyes of a prisoner condemned for having loved. Jaya was a strange season inscribed on the destiny of man.

Absence bares a state of freedom, a frightening freedom. Absence imprisons you in an open jail. It bestows on you the privilege of recreating this world of staid habits and meanings and with the same sleight of hand, also confers on you a blindness which prevents you from seeing all that you recreate. It gives you the kingdom but not the eyes to admire your queen. With absence, your planet is born anew, but this planet is also a creation which denies the being of its own creator. It is an illusion, it is non-history. It is and it is not. Nothing matters for nothing is. For deep in the distance, on the tongue of the horizon, Ganga shall flow and, on her, my solitary boat shall pose the eternal question: 'Who am I? Who is she? Why is she here and not here? Why has she gone and yet not gone? Where is the **Laxman Jhoola,** the bridge over two desires?' If only I could flow like Ganga into the bosom of the infinite seas...

On my way back from the airport, exhausted by the swells of my mind, I walked into a small garden off Avenue du Maine. I stretched myself on the lawns. Two children, around seven or eight, were sitting arm in arm on a parched green bench. The girl had a poster in her hand with pictures of actors and actresses in different film costumes. On top, it said: guess who is who? The little girl, Armelle, said musingly: 'When I grow up, I'll date this actor. How handsome he is!' The young boy, Jean, took his turn: 'When I grow up, I'll date this girl. She's so pretty!' And so they carried on playfully, dating an actor or an actress on the chess-board of unfettered desires. Suddenly the girl screamed in triumph: 'And I'll date him. That's it, I've won...' The boy was stunned, sad, for the poster had no women left to date any more. He turned abruptly and rushed to hide himself in the pleats of his mother's skirt. *Maman* said: 'Come, come, it's getting late, children. Let's go before it gets dark.' The little boy, looking wonderingly at the sun, asked: 'Maman, why does the sun ever set...?'

I reached home and turned the key gently to enter a temple or a cemetery, I didn't know what. I moved to pick up a packet of cigarettes and found an envelope addressed to me. Thus spoke Jaya: *'These fourteen days with you have left little more to desire of life. I would accomplish my karma if, in the next birth, we could spend three days on the banks of Ganga in Benares. May you be loved to the point of madness. Your mad Jaya...'*

I walked out of the studio and sat on the steps of the staircase. A strong wind was whistling down the stairwell. I looked down. Some fifty steps below, angry waves of Ganga were lashing the jagged shores of history. Powerful drafts of monsoon wind made the bathers uneasy. The women giggled and laughed as they tried to clutch the fluttering cottons on their tanned bodies. The fishermen, their nets suspended from water logs, were rocking endlessly. And right under my eyes, on the *Ram Ghat* in Benares, a young woman, dressed in red as she was for her wedding, was enveloped in yellow flames, surrounded by the incessant chanting of '*Rama nama satya hai, Rama nama satya hai.*' The sound of the funeral dirge rose high, as it had for the funeral of Che Guevara. A little girl floated a lamp on the waves, thanking Ganga for introducing her to death at the dainty age of seven. Amidst all these earthly emotions, Ganga, indifferent and omnipresent, flowed timelessly, an interminable black sheet of velvet offered to the destiny of India.

Thus Jaya became Ganga and Ganga, Jaya. Before me, Ganga threw her arms wide open and I walked into them just as I had into those of Jaya. Jaya, then, had become this long skirting pilgrimage down the waters which joined the glaciers of the Himalayas to the evaporating mirages of the Bay of Bengal. Jaya, for me, had reincarnated herself as this long and ancient river along the banks of which *the Vedas*, the *Puranas*, the *Mahabharata* and the *Ramayana* took their venerated births. By the early hours of the morning, Jaya had become this river-civilisation, whose bosom carried the footprints of each pilgrim of Indian history. From the Aryans to the Mauryas, from the Kushans to the Guptas, from the Central Asians to the Persians, from the Mughals to the British, each paid Ganga the homage that was her due. By the twentieth century, Jaya, she has already spun together religiosity and heresy, faith and greed, devotion and crime, the disturbing poetry of her nomad-singers and the facile commercialism of Indian cinema. Just as I had accepted Jaya despite the threat of madness, I accepted Ganga, her reincarnation, with all her philosophical truths and historical blasphemies. For above all, Jaya was the timeless flow of Ganga, a vein on a slender pelican-neck in which ran the purple breath of all humanity.

'Watch out pretty wave, there is a swarm of photons beneath your skirt!' I raised the edge of her skirt, and discovered Ganga, the *Vedic* hymn, Ganga, the *anjana-timira-bhanu*, light in the darkness of ignorance, Ganga, the poetry of Kabir, Mira and Surdas, Ganga, the anti-symphony of the Bauls and Majhis of Bengal, Ganga, the criminal and Ganga, the courtesan.

One Sunday morning, in an autumn crying colour, I packed my bags and left for Ganga.

Gangotri

SEVERAL WEEKS AWAY FROM THAT WET AUTUMNAL memory, I was deep into the bosom of the Himalayas. The Bhagirathi, the real ancestor of Ganga, at Lanka, a little village below Gangotri, looked playful and coquettish. Her gushing waters made their turbulent course through a finely sculptured gorge, and then slipped imperceptibly into a large crystalline pool of turquoise water. To the left was the Jharhganga, one of the many Gangas in the region. Bouncing and cart-wheeling over the rocks, her waters flowed feverishly into Mother Bhagirathi, knowing well that it was here at Lanka that they dissolved their identity in the universal might of the holy river.

Some hundred metres above the river, stood two black poles on opposite banks, announcing the most memorable fact of Ganga's autobiography. It was by means of these poles and the long jute ropes suspended from their tops that the pilgrim of ancient times could swing himself across the river and take the perilous path that led to the mysterious source of the sacred river. The rope bridge was an accidental monument, neglected and long forgotten, in memory of those pilgrims, who with cloth-bundles on their backs and bamboo-umbrellas in their hands, had slipped from the ropes to find salvation in the roaring currents of the Bhagirathi. The rope bridge was also a reminder that the Gangotri ya*tra* to the source of the holy river was indeed a rare penance hazarded only by those who had abandoned their desire to exist on this planet of hypocrisy and greed. So, expectedly, a large mass of pilgrims admitted defeat before the frightening gaze of Gangetic ropeways, and retraced their steps towards the plains. The deathless—they gambled their lives in the name of a blind faith; and those who were still prisoners of the five vices of Hinduism, contented themselves with a quick dip at Lanka, before hurrying back to the worldly warmth of their homes. If not a complete *moksha*, it was at least a semi-*moksha*, for they had better gods to worship.

The times have changed since. For the Gangotri pilgrim, the last major landmark was the Indo-Chinese war of 1962. In the wake of a humiliating defeat at the hands of China, India roared: 'They've provoked a sleeping tiger.' The proud tiger woke up to the sordid nightmare that, let alone sophisticated weaponry, he did not even have enough roads and vehicles to reach the frontiers where a war was being fought between the 'red ants' and the Nehruite advocates of the Panchashila. The tiger then decided to let his poor mind their poor, and promptly prepared to fortify Indian defences through unaffordable arms deals and intense construction activity in the mountains. Gangotri pilgrim was thus an indirect and charmed beneficiary of a much larger geo-political game of international boundaries. A handful of years ago, the pilgrim had to walk almost 150 kilometres up puzzling mountain pathways amidst harsh weather. Now, the dubious boon of modern warfare had brought him a bare twenty-eight kilometres from the origin of the sacred Bhagirathi.

Lugging a weighty bag on my shoulder, I walked up to the end of a gravel track. The bag had really begun to annoy me. I had left Paris in a rush. Fevered in love, searching for the source of Jaya, probing the roots of my own soul, I had dumped all sorts of things into a large shoulder bag. The little wheels under it had served me quite well on several occasions, but here,

3000 metres above the sea-level, in the midst of steep climbs and slippery pathways, my 'diplomat' bag was nothing short of a millstone round the neck.

I opened the bag to see what I could dispense with. The more I rummaged through it, the more I realised what I had forgotten to bring along. Since there was no choice before me, I lifted the bag and started walking across the half-constructed bridge which linked the mainland to the track leading to the source of the holy river. I noticed two young inhabitants of the region seated against the backdrop of an election poster. Their pahari banter came slicing through the thick *beedi* smoke.

'*Namaskar, bhaiya,*' I greeted them. They looked at me, puzzled. I greeted them again, but they didn't respond.

'Can you tell me the way to Gangotri please?' I asked.

'You mean the Gangotri temple?'

'Yes.'

'But there's no point in going there.'

'Why? I am a pilgrim.'

'The temple is closed. This is off-season. It'll open in the summer. Come again with the other pilgrims.' They sounded too abrupt and rude to be Paharis, as the hillfolk are usually quite kind and hospitable.

Turning away, they started chattering and laughing.

'But how do I get to Gangotri?' I persisted.

'We've told you, haven't we? *Vahan ulloo bolte hein*, it's a land of owls these days. There's no point in going there.' They looked at me strangely, as if suspecting my sanity, and asserted:

'There are no priests, no attendants, no beds, no food, there's nothing. What will you do among hooting owls?'

'*Are Baba*, just tell me how to get to Gangotri. The rest is up to me.'

'Don't bother about him. He's probably mad.' They looked

at each other and laughed, as if sharing a private joke.

'May I have a glass of water?' I was thirsty.

'We don't have glasses here. This is not a restaurant,' one of them retorted rudely.

'But could I have some water, anyway?'

'Go down to the river.'

They gaped at me incredulously, then exchanged a glance with each other, and burst out laughing again. Fed up with their non-sense, I picked up my bag and crossed the river, walking carefully on the steel girders of the incomplete bridge. As I stood puzzled before two tracks that led up the mountain, one of the two cheeky Paharis shouted from the back: 'Go right for Gangotri.' The other added: 'And follow the hooting of the owls. It will take to the temple…'

I reached the top, a bit breathless. Physical exhaustion made the trees appear blurred and hazy. I heard some rustling in the thickets. A short drooping man, wearing torn black pyjamas and a pair of army boots that slanted like a beret at the heels, walked out of the forest. He was carrying a bundle of fuel wood in his hands. Almost involuntarily, I cried out, *'Bhaiya*, could I have some water please?' Without uttering a word, a yes or a no, he disappeared behind the layers of *deodar* trees, stroking tree-trunks along the way as if he were playing a harp. The sound of the local Pahari song he was humming gradually faded away as he receded into the distance. A few minutes later, he returned with a pot of water, colder than ice.

'What are you doing here in the snow and ice?' He asked, pouring out some water into my cupped hand.

'I am going to Gaumukh, the source of Ganga.'

'But this is not the season. The temple is shut.'

'Well, seasons belong to the mind, don't they?' I smiled at him, but he did not have a clue as to what I was saying.

'It's not going to be easy,' he warned me. 'Everything is shut.'

'That doesn't worry me. It's this damned weight on my shoulder that's bothering me.'

'What weight? This little bundle? Come on, *sahib*, this is nothing. A child of seven can carry this in these parts. You should have come during the season. You could have hired a jeep.'

'A jeep?'

'You surely know what a jeep is, *sahib*.'

'Yes, of course. But how the hell do they get the jeeps across? There's not even a bridge in place yet!'

'But there are jeeps here. They've been around for years, since the last war. Rich merchants from the plains buy them in army auctions. They bring the jeeps up to the other end of the road, dismantle them completely, get them across the river and reassemble them again on this end. One trip to Gangotri costs seventy rupees. It's the greatest business going in these parts. They make *lakhs* each season. So you see, it would be better if you came during the season.' Scarcely had he finished his word of advice than he blew his nose into his hand and pasted a rich dose of mucus on the trunk of a lovely pine, which had served as his harp a minute ago.

'What do you do?' I asked.

'I work for a *seth* who lives in Uttarkashi. I set up tea-stalls for him—odd jobs, bring wood from the forest, chop it to size, put it together, make huts... I have a lot of work. It has to be completed before the pilgrim season begins. When the season starts, someone from the *seth's* family will come and run the shop.'

'And you? What will do you?'

'I work as a porter during the season. There was good money in it earlier, but these days the jeeps have pushed our rates down to thirty rupees a trip.' He suddenly turned towards the west: 'The sunrays are slanting. You'd better be on your way.'

'But wouldn't you like to come along with me?' I tried to tempt him. 'I'll employ you as my porter. It will be fun. You can tell me about life in the mountains—how you live, work, eat ...'

'What's there to say about life in the mountains? It's cold, wet, and horrible. But tell me, *sahib*, where exactly do you want to go?'

'Gaumukh or Gangotri. You decide.'

The prospect of off-season employment started to work on the porter and he became thoughtful. He lit a *beedi*, and after a few minutes of silence, muttered:

'What about him?'

'About whom?'

'The *seth*.'

'Come on, it's only for a day. You'll be back tomorrow. One day is not asking for too much.'

'It might be risky... No, I don't think I can accompany you. It's asking for trouble.'

I picked up my bag and started walking. Realising that I was not playing his game, he called out aloud: 'Tell me, *sahib*, how much are you willing to pay?' I needed him so desperately that I was prepared to give him anything within my means. I offered him one hundred rupees, three times his normal wage. He turned it down: 'Life is so costly these days. What can you buy with a hundred rupee note?' 'A hundred and fifty then?' I upped the amount. He grumbled for a while and then picked up the bag and muttered: 'But I'll only go up to Gangotri. For this sum, I can't go to Gaumukh.' I accepted. With my bag slung over his head, Ram Bahadur was soon trotting a good hundred meters ahead of me. He seemed to have been born with a fifty-kilo weight on his back.

The sky looked clean blue—the blue of a woman's love-bite. Silenced by the overpowering beauty of the Himalayas, we walked for well over an hour before catching a first glimpse of Gangotri. A cluster of some hundred houses, their architecture blurred by the mist of a restless Bhagirathi, made it seem as if a child had scrawled a village in his drawing-book. Gangotri was deserted. Not a soul in sight. The houses were locked and sealed with red and saffron strips of cloth: Each pilgrim's lodge announced the name of the region whose pilgrims it welcomed. An air of abandon and death loomed over Gangotri and yet, the holy village emanated a peculiar spiritual force. The tiny triangular white flags, the staccato of their flapping and the frenzied music of Bhagirathi bestowed on this ancient village of Hindu belief a mysterious immortality. Just as Gangotri reinforced belief in the endless cycle of reincarnations, it itself appeared to be the product of infinite cycles of life and death. With its abandoned huts and deserted temples, dead and yet immortal, Gangotri described a circularity over life and death.

We crossed the bridge over Kedarganga, another tributary of the Bhagirathi, when Ram Bahadur knocked at the door of a hut which in the outlandish surroundings of the Himalayas resembled an alpine chalet. A short and stout young man of about thirty, holding a kerosene lamp in one hand and a butcher's knife in the other, opened the door. He smelt of onion and garlic. Shifting his gaze from the porter to me, he smiled warmly. From his hospitable glance I knew I would not have to freeze to death that night.

'Can you put me up for the night? I am...'

'Yes, yes, welcome *sahib*. You're most welcome. This is an inspection bungalow.' I thanked heaven for creating bureaucrats and ministers on this earth for, otherwise, there would neither be inspections nor inspection bungalows to house wayward pilgrims like me.

'What's your name?' I asked my friendly host.

'Ram Bahadur, *sahib*.'

'My name is Nishant.'

'Have you come from Dehradun, *sahib?*'

'No, no. I've come from Paris. Have you heard of Paris?'

'Oh yes. A very long time ago I saw a Hindi film called *An Evening in Paris*. Lovely city. Paris too has a Qutub Minar.'

'Yes, if you like. A Qutub Minar for New Delhi and an Eiffel Tower for Paris.'

'Is he your servant?' he asked, pointing towards the porter.

'No, he is a porter from Bhaironghati. He is also called Ram Bahadur.'

'O *sahib*, there are so many *paharis* with this name.'

Ram Bahadur is a very common name among the Nepalese Gurkhas. In fact, in India, for any Gurkha who comes in from Nepal, there is just one name: 'Bahadur'. Bahadur means the brave one, but over the years, the Nepali migrant, rugged and tough, has earned the reputation of being not only a good fighter but also someone who is 'mindlessly faithful' and 'unflinchingly loyal'. It is this dual trait among the innocent inhabitants of the Nepal Himalayas that gave them easy entry into the British Indian Army. Again, it was not altogether an accident that Maggie Thatcher sent out the Nepalese Gurkha regiments to fight her modern colonial war in the Falklands.

Ram Bahadur opened the doors to unbelievable comfort: a room, a large soft bed, clean sheets, a quilt and a kerosene lamp. Accustomed to the caste and class hierarchies of the Indian elite, Ram Bahadur left me to the vagaries of my humour and silently retreated to prepare a make-shift dinner. The other Ram Bahadur, the porter, was already on the road back home, if ever he had one...

I lit the kerosene lamp, took out my diary and thought of scribbling a few lines in it. 'I've just stepped into a marvellous chalet at Gangotri. It's night. Quiet, a divine quiet which I've never experienced before. It's not a quiet which comes from the negation of sound, but, strangely, from a certain kind of sound which only a river in the mountains can produce. Yes, Ganga proves that the purest silence is a sound.

A lullaby, Ganga grows on me like a smooth wine, dissolving the real into the self. Ganga tip-toes gently into the mind, and there she builds in it, layer by layer, a sandbed of harmony which is the only promise she can offer to the horrors of history. She invokes a unique nostalgia. She makes me believe in a past that never was, a future that will never be.

Hey, Jaya, where are you? So present and so absent. Can you hear Ganga? Do you agree that nothing heals better than a constant rhythm?'

I noticed a bright yellow glow coming in from the back of the cottage. I walked out. Bahadur had lit a small fire. The firewood was humid. It wept as it burnt.

Agni rekindled in me the desire for Jaya. Was it not on the first night when she lay beside me that I had dreamt of a magnificent golden bush-fire? The fire reduced the healing touch of Ganga to ashes and consummated the unruly, the mad. The flames welcomed me teasingly towards the game of suicide; they sucked me in just when I wanted to be sucked in the most. Just then Bahadur came and announced that dinner was ready. 'Please leave the food on the table, Bahadur. I'll help myself.'

I got up and reached for my bag. Caution rang in my ears for, beyond Rishikesh, alcohol is taboo. In Gangotri it is even sacrilege. Like many others before me, I too was a pilgrim to the mysterious birth of this divinity and I bowed low before her unchallenged might, but I had my own gods to please and my own ends to reach. I pulled out my bottle of rum. Swirling, stumbling and humming *bhajans,* I walked out into the arms of a jet-black night. Above, the sky was meticulously lit, each star in its place giving a providential guard of honour to a pilgrim who had dared heresy in the imperial courts of Goddess Ganga. As I stared deep into her bosom, I noticed that the night resembled my mother, my youthful mother, in a light black veil studded with golden stars, the veil with which my mother carried herself through the severest glances of a bourgeois evening. My mother looked into the mirror, she saw Jaya. Jaya looked into the mirror, she saw *Ma*. *Ma* was Jaya, Jaya was Ganga, and Ganga, *Ma*. With all oedipal truths thus complete, I moved, bottle still in hand, towards the historic temple of Gangotri.

'*Sahib, sahib.*' Someone called out to me. It was dark.

'Yes. Who's it?'

'It's me. Bahadur.'

'What…'

'*Sahib, sahib,*' he pleaded. 'What are you doing?'

'Nothing.'

'*Sahib,* come, the dinner is ready.'

'Yes, Bahadur, I'll be back soon. I must visit the temple before we eat.'

'*Sahib,* what are you doing?' He had obviously noticed the bottle of rum in my hand.

'Nothing, I am just going to the temple.

'No, *sahib.* Have some respect for the temple. Don't!'

'If I didn't have respect, Bahadur, I wouldn't have taken the pain to come this far. I'll be back soon.'

'*Sahib, sahib.* This is sacrilege, *sahib.*' His words of caution dissolved in the star-lit night.

Source

I WOKE UP WITH BAHADUR KNOCKING AT THE DOOR. HE greeted me into the morning with a steaming cup of *Kangra* tea and gently placed a bucket of hot water in the bathroom. Rubbing his hands vigorously, he muttered:

'So your programme is all upset?'

'Why?'

'Haven't you looked out of the window?'

It had snowed heavily. Everything around me was white, blinding white. Trees, bridges, housetops, stones, everything was covered in thick, soft snow. Out in the bungalow compound, the washing line looked like a thread of snow sparkling in the morning sun. There was not a soul in sight. Even the birds had not dared come out of their nests for their dawn cacophony. Deep in the distance, the Gangotri temple was wrapped in sheets of snow, strangely resembling St. Francois de Sales, an old church in Annemasse, in the French Alps.

'Gangotri looks beautiful,' I remarked.

'Yes, *sahib,* beautiful to look at but not otherwise. The track to Gaumukh must be blocked. The mountains here are not like those in Ladakh. The hills tend to crumble in the rain. There are frequent landslides and accidents. And to reach Gaumukh, good weather is essential. It's a long walk. I don't think you should risk it today.'

'Do you really think so?'

'Yes, I don't think you should leave today.'

'But the sun holds promise.'

'The weather in the mountains is treacherous, *sahib*. I suggest you wait for a couple of days. After all, Gaumukh is a good eighteen kilometres away, and doing the journey in a day is not going to be very simple.' Having warned me amply, Bahadur retreated into the kitchen to prepare breakfast.

I wanted to heed his warning but, for some inexplicable reason, I could not see myself postponing my programme for the fear of some imaginary landslide. My father had once told me: 'I don't mind, my son, if you die of a snake-bite, but I'd hate it if you died of the fear of a snake-bite.' This little remark conveyed that we were Rajputs, the 'warrior' caste, whose principal business in Hindu society seems to have been to fight wars over land and women. Quite apart from this inspiration of a proud Rajput father, I was in a fearless state of mind. I had nothing to defend, nothing to lose; life had been reduced to a meaningless gamble, and was it not better to gamble it away in the anonymity of the Himalayas than at the altar of a world which did not even hold out to me the promise of a decent cremation?

Ram Bahadur reluctantly charted out my route. The only *ashram*, a pilgrims' lodge, was some fifteen kilometres away. A short distance before this *ashram*, there was normally another place for a night-halt, but it was closed during winter. Bahadur assured me, however, that there would certainly be someone at the *Lal Baba Ashram*, three kilometres short of Gaumukh. The *ashram* was run by a kind and renowned *sadhu*, who offered courtesy to all pilgrims. 'And then, you're from Paris,' added Bahadur cheekily, 'they'll be even more hospitable to you!'

All alone, accompanied intermittently by my shadow, I was deep in the intriguing labyrinths of the Himalayas. On my right, the tops of the mountain ranges were lined by tall *deodar* trees.

Their smooth trunks, swaying in the gentle breeze and black against the midday sun, resembled the fine arched eye-lashes of the Himalayan Goddess, Ganga, who, some 500 metres below, was roaring in a jagged gorge. The birds chirped around me but their beautiful song was masked by a sentiment of emptiness. The sight of numerous caves, charred with smoke and littered with rusted household paraphernalia, only accentuated the sentiment of solitude, as even the *sadhus* seemed to have abandoned the tracks to which I had condemned myself for a curious pilgrimage. My feet were cold. My gait echoed like the sound of purposelessness. With each step into the void, a hundred questions haunted my mind: 'Who was I? What was I doing in the Himalayas? Where was I heading? What for, and why?' An occasional leaf or a twig fell from a tree and I knew the world still existed around me, otherwise there was no movement. There were not even any road-markings to tell how deep I had penetrated into the Himalayan womb, and it was frightening to think of the distance I had come from a world which measured its existence on the road maps of space and on the electronic-dials of time. The force of solitude was indeed frightening, and if there was anything that could stop it from consuming me, it was the intrinsic beauty of silence.

I noticed faint footprints on the snow. Tiny, roundish, flat-footed, the marks were fresh, melting along their edges. Although I could see no-one around, I was convinced there was someone ahead, someone whose destiny was sculpted with the same pain as mine. A sudden hope erupted in me, a desire to meet someone who, like me, had survived the holocaust on this earth. I started walking faster. The track was narrow and slippery and I realised that I was walking much too fast. Below, the roaring current of the Bhagirathi waited to swallow me. Impatient to meet my invisible fellow-traveller, I continued to follow the footprints.

They disappeared to reappear again; they climbed up; they climbed down. At times, the footprint was so vivid that I could virtually see the design on the sole of the shoe and, yet, there were times when the trace was so faint and withered that it evoked the claws of some dreadful animal. I noticed the footprints turn towards a cave. At first, the foul-smelling, dark hole made me hesitate, but the urge for human contact was so compelling that I decided to enter the cave. A stale, putrid smell filled the cave; two rusted tin canisters, an oil bottle with dead earthworms, a long bone and a brass bell lent the atmosphere a touch of the sinister. Just as I was leaving, I noticed grease-stained paper which had probably been used to pack some *parathas*. The paper still carried the smell of food. I returned to my track with the certitude that there was another human companion on his way to Gaumukh. The footprints continued to play hide and seek until they disappeared with the fading light. Before the swells of solitude could submerge me again, the adumbral geometry of the *Lal Baba Ashram* rose before my eyes.

Lal Baba Ashram, as Bahadur had explained earlier in the morning, was the only halt on the way to Gaumukh. Regardless of the snowy seasons, *Lal Baba* ensured permanent hospitality at his *ashram*. His house was open to all; the poor or the sick, the needy or the wealthy, the diseased or the healthy, all slept for once under a roof which rejected the class and caste distinctions of society. In return for the service that *Lal Baba* had rendered the religious world, wealthy pilgrims over the years had donated enough to create sufficient resources for a comfortable running of the *ashram*. *Lal Baba*, Bahadur had told me, saw to it personally that no one went hungry or without a shelter. Tired and exhausted after a long journey, a pilgrim could not hope to arrive at a more welcome threshold.

From a distance the *ashram* resembled a helipad with three

barracks constructed around a flat, square piece of land. The heavy pinewood doors were flung wide open and the evening wind whistled through the *ashram*, making its tin-sheet roofs shiver and rattle. There was no-one in sight. I greeted the invisible saint: 'Jai Ram ji ki, baba. Jai Ram ji ki.' A lazy, drawling reply came from behind me: 'Jai Ram ji ki'. I turned around and saw *baba* — wheat-complexioned, large bulging eyes, a broad forehead, a wise beard, long flowing hair, an axe in his hand. Overwhelmed to see him, I walked towards him, greeted him again and, without the slightest hesitation, touched his feet with reverence. He smiled tenderly.

'I've heard so much about you, *baba*'. My voice choked with emotion. 'Everyone in the mountains sings your praises! To spend decades in solitude in the biting cold itself makes you a *mahatma*.' I could not but be honest about my feelings. Shy, *baba* was a shade overcome by my outspoken compliment. Slightly embarrassed, he murmured: 'I'm sorry to disappoint you, *bhaiya*, but I am not *Lal baba*. He has gone to Calcutta. He does not stay here in the winters. He doesn't like the cold.'

'But I was told *Lal Baba* stays here through the year.'

'Whoever told you that! He can't stand the winter in the mountains. Well before the first snow, he leaves for the plains. Then, he has other things to attend to... Calcutta, Benares, Gaya. He moves around a lot. Depends on his meetings with the officers and ministers...'

'And you? Are you one of his disciples?'

'No, no. I am an employee. I look after his *ashram* through the winters.'

'You mean he gives you a salary, like in any other job.'

'Not really. *Baba* is a gentle soul. He gives me food, shelter, clothing, and some food to carry back for the family.'

'And the family, where do they live?'

'Down in Uttarkashi. You must have crossed it on your way up.'

'Yes, I did.'

'Tell me, were there a lot of landslides and rain around Uttarkashi?'

'No. It was fairly dry.'

'Thank God! I was quite worried about them. We have a little hut at the foot of a hill and when it rains, it gets quite dangerous.'

'Have you been here long?'

'Four months.' Dropping the axe on the ground, he added with a mix of anxiety and irritation: 'My wife and kids are at home. I hope there's enough to eat. If only someone could come and relieve me...'

'And when will *baba* return?'

'When the season begins and the pilgrims start arriving.' Pratap, *Lal Baba's* deputy for the winter months, led me into the *ashram* compound. As I sat on the edge of a rectangular stone which felt like a slab of ice, Pratap noticed that I was cold and fetched me a blanket. A glass of tea, scented with a local herb, was enough to make me feel at home.

'Where are you from?' asked Pratap.

'Well, from a place pretty far from here.'

'You're from the plains, aren't you?'

'Yes. From a place called Paris.'

'What did you say?'

'Paris.'

'Paris? Strange, never heard of the place.' He twisted and turned the name 'Paris' three or four times in his mouth and then said musingly: 'People come here from all over the world, but I've never heard of this place. What did you say? Palis? Palis? Never heard of it.'

Instead of torturing him with lessons in elementary geography, I explained that Paris was a city close to New Delhi. 'Oh, Delhi!' exclaimed Pratap, 'Who doesn't know Delhi! The *durbar!* Now with the new track laid, a lot of people come from Delhi. In the good old days, it was tough coming here. Thirty out of a hundred pilgrims got swept away by landslides. And now, even Indira Gandhi can come! She came here last season. Tell me, did you have a good journey?'

'Not too bad. A bit tiring.'

'I'll get the food ready. The sun's already behind the hills. Eat, then you can go to sleep.'

Pratap got up slowly, rubbed his hands on his *pyjamas* and with a heavy gait, walked towards the kitchen. There was still enough light to jot down a few lines in my diary. 'I've just met a man called Pratap at *Lal Baba's ashram.* His gestures reveal the entire universe of old civilisations. The slow movements, the majestic turn of the hand, the lazy, bumpy laughter, each gesture of this man indicates a certain being of 'time' that India lives in the deep recesses of its countryside. It is this 'time', untouched by the revolutions of our era, which demarcates the East from the civilisations of the West. Time lives in speech, in gestures, in glances, in imperceptible facial movements, in each pore of human behaviour, and it is in this sense that Pratap becomes the revealing point of an entire culture which disappears each day with the ticking of electronic time. Pratap's languid movements, like those of a wise banyan tree, reveal an inner harmony. I said to him this evening: "You don't talk much, Pratap *bhaiya.*" "What's there to say?' he answered with absurd laughter, and then looked away into the horizon, completely unmindful of the big ant which promenaded freely on the wrinkles of his forehead.'

It was getting cold outside. I took off my shoes and entered the kitchen. Pratap was sitting on his haunches before the mud oven. The wood was damp, its flame not quite a full burst of yellow. In the flickering glow, I noticed that Pratap had lovely features and even lovelier eyes, which reflected the entire oven, the fire and the pot, on their shining irises. By his side stood stacks and stacks of wood, an inexhaustible stock of fuel, good enough to last many seasons of snow and cold. 'Oh no!' Pratap remarked, 'This is just about enough for a month! It's cold and we rely on wood for everything.' The *dal* had begun to boil in the huge brass pot and the rice was done. Pratap rinsed the aluminium *thalis* with warm water and served me some *dal* and rice and green chillies to add sting to food which, in the absence of spices in the deep Himalayas, tends to be bland. More than the quality of food or cooking, it was the simplicity and the art of serving that lent this meal a flavour of maternal nostalgia.

Fatigue from the long day's walk was descending on me. My eyelids felt heavy and each part of my body, bones and muscles, ached intensely. Seeing me drop off to sleep on my haunches, Pratap said with concern: 'Please don't bother with the dishes. Come with me, I'll show you your bed.'

A tiny oil lamp showing us the way, Pratap led me to a small hut behind the kitchen. So as not to abandon me completely to the gods of darkness, he found me a small candle, the size of a *cornichon*, and placed it carefully on a ledge protruding from the wall. I lit the candle–and *Lal Baba's* horrors came alive. The mattress was filthy black and the quilt so badly stained that I could literally peel a sheet of grime off its covers. A large piece of cloth, whose actual shape was anywhere between a triangle and a rectangle and a circle, and which was in all likelihood to serve as my bed-sheet, was filled with dubious stains which made me wonder if these sheets belonged to the sexually-starved soldiers patrolling the Indo-Chinese frontiers. The smell of stale, damp linen and the devotional fragrance of the Gaumukh pilgrims, was heady enough to scare a butcher and, just above my head, was a large hole in the roof, stuffed with some plastic bags, through the sides of which snow, rain and wind could all enter to remind the pilgrim that, on such ascetic *yatras*, he could not afford to loll in comfort. The prospect of sleep looked bleak, but I was really too tired to harbour the dreams of a five-star tourist. I was ready to slip into bed, when I noticed two over-nourished insomniac cockroaches playing hide and seek on my mattress. I wielded my 'Adidas' as a weapon but, as their luck would have it, the candle called it a day. I was all set to sleep when Pratap arrived:

'It's rather cold and windy outside,' he warned, 'I suggest you keep the door bolted.'

'Thanks, *bhaiya*, I'll bolt it.'

'Don't bother! Don't bother getting up, there's no bolt inside.' he said apologetically. 'Let me latch it from the outside and I'll wake you up for the morning prayers.'

I shut my eyes.

My breathing is not smooth. I fear my asthma is back. It's getting worse every minute. Pratap says he has a special herbal therapy for me. He lights me a few foul-smelling herbs and asks me to inhale the smoke. Smoke makes it worse. I protest, but Pratap insists that I inhale deeply. I'm dizzy, my head is spinning. I can't breathe. Pratap's face has changed; his eyes look wild, his face mad. I'm convinced Pratap is up to some mischief. This herb is a trap: he wants to poison me. I'm gasping for breath. His hands cut through the cloud of smoke and grab me by my neck. 'Pratap! Pratap Bhaiya! What are you …' He begins to strangle me. I dig my nails into his hands. He tightens the hold and knocks my head against the wall…

I woke up with a start. I was sweating and gasping for air. For the first few seconds, I couldn't figure out what was happening and then, I realised that it was not just a nightmare. There was smoke in the room, and no oxygen. Smoke, smoke and more smoke... I dashed for the door, choked. The door was locked. I pulled hard but it was firmly latched. I couldn't breathe; it was becoming unbearable. I banged and banged at the door and called out for Pratap. No answer. I called out again, without success. Pulling at the door with renewed force, I managed to break the latch. I rushed out towards the main gate, but only managed to knock something down in the dark which made a pile of utensils tumble and clatter. There was still no sign of Pratap.

Once I managed to reach the doorstep, the air was fresh and icy. The lungs began to breathe again and the eyes recovered their focus. A strong wind whistled through the mountains and the snowfall tapped gently on the tin-sheet roof. As I sat impatiently waiting for the morning that refused to arrive, Pratap appeared from somewhere at the back and in a voice completely uninformed of my agonies, asked, 'Why are you up so early, *bhaiya*? It's not yet time for the morning prayer.'

The nightmare over, feeling more exhausted on waking than on going to bed, I prepared to leave for Gaumukh. Pratap insisted that I wait for the weather to clear, but I stuck to my decision, preferring the icy dangers of Gaumukh to the warmth of his asphyxiating nights. A hot cup of tea, some *dal* and rice, and I was back on the track.

I had not been on the path for long when I noticed the footprints again. The same foot, the same size, the same shape. The snow being fresh, the mark was deeper and clearer. Re-enacting the absurd drama of the day before, the footprints walked into a dark cave, depositing yet another greasy paper which smelt of food and, then, walked out on to the track without leaving any further trace of their identity. Before the suspense could absorb me any further, there was a fork in the track. The footprints turned left. I followed them until the mystery of the footsteps metamorphosed into a divine apparition before my eyes.

Dressed in a *salwar-kameez*, a shawl tied tightly around her head, kneeling, eyes shut, completely oblivious of my presence, a young girl was praying. Before her earthly pleadings, Gaumukh was a gaping dark tunnel in a colossal glacier: gigantic, immovable, godly. Bruise-blue ice lined the orifice, a misty projectile of water gushed out of it with amazing force. The wide open mouth and the long, turquoise tongue of water gave Gaumukh the look of a god, who was sadistically poking fun at pilgrims who had hoped to pay their ultimate homage to Ganga at its place of birth. If anything, Gaumukh told its weary pilgrim that Goddess Ganga was never born: She had always been and shall always be.

The sun had just come out, its rays blinding the eye. Curious to know the other pilgrim, I walked up to the girl discreetly.

'*Namaskar, behan,*' I greeted her.

'*Adaabarzhai, bhaijaan,*' she replied in Urdu. Her spontaneous hand-gesture betrayed she was Muslim.

'Gaumukh looks beautiful in the morning sun' Surprised by my remark, she asked:

'Are you a tourist?'

'No, not really. Well... a pilgrim, I suppose.' It must have been something in my manner for she asked me with deep concern:

'*Allah Mian ki dua se ghar mein khairiyat to hai*, By the grace of Allah, I hope everything is well at home' She sounded so grown-up!

'Yes, and with you?'

'*Amma* is in hospital.' Her glance dropped.

'What happened?'

'Cancer. I have come to seek a boon from Ganga*ma*.' Her voice filled with pain.

I put a hand on her shoulder with affection and tried to cheer her up with mundane questions.

'You're not wearing enough for this weather.'
'Yes, it's quite cold.'
'Where are you from?'
'From Meerut.'
'And your name?'
'Shabnam.' *Shabnam*, the morning dew.
'Have you come alone?' I asked.
'My uncle brought me up to Lanka. He is waiting there for me. My father insisted that I do the last part of the pilgrimage all alone.'
'Don't you have any brothers and sisters?'
'Yes, a brother and a sister. Both older.'
'Why didn't your brother come for the pilgrimage, then?'
'Oh, it's a long story! My father dreamt that he should send his youngest daughter for a Gangotri *yatra*.' She spoke Urdu with a poetic sonority. The phonemes of this language, a rare mix of Persian, Arabic and Hindi, are indeed so musical that even ordinary comments of daily life sound as metaphors of a poem. Suddenly, Shabnam broke the silence and remarked:
'You must wonder why a Muslim girl is on a Hindu pilgrimage.'
'I hadn't really thought of that.'
'You see, *amma* is a Hindu and my father, a Muslim. My father dreamt that only Ganga, the Hindu goddess, could cure my mother. So I was sent here.'
'What does your father do, Shabnam?'
'He is a poet. My mother too was a poetess.'
'Was?'
'Oh! She's very sick. It's going to be difficult for her...'
Her voice choked with emotion and a film of pain floated over her eyes. I took the bulky cloth-bag off her shoulder and, slowly, started heading towards Gangotri. Shabnam chose to maintain a solemn silence. As we trudged along, accompanied

by our shadows extending into the west, Ganga chanted her magical *mantras* in the deep gorges of the Himalayas. There was a silent bond between us. Words were replaced by two speechless presences; the gait of our staggering feet was the only sound of our mutual affection. It felt as though we had known each other for ages. Nothing befriends the most distant of strangers as a common pain. Happiness cannot be shared, but pain can.

Shabnam broke the silence with a chuckle: 'I was thinking of my childhood. About *amma* and me. You know, *bhaijaan*, we used to stay in this little house. We had rented two tiny rooms in a poor suburb of Meerut. Since there was no fan at home, we would pull the cots out into the street at night. Well, you know how, in summer, everyone sleeps outside. At bedtime, *amma* used to tell me stories from the *Ramayana* and the *Mahabharata*. I was just thinking about the story she told me about *Gangama*. My mother had a way of relating which made it so easy to remember the tales...'

'What story were you thinking of, Shabnam?'

She smirked and said: 'And what awful neighbours we had! You know, *bhaijaan*, the neighbours sleeping in the street were all Muslims and they didn't like my mother telling me about Hindu gods and goddesses. They felt that since she had married a Muslim, she should now forget her Hindu past. But my father respected my mother's beliefs. Tell me, *bhaijaan*, did your mother tell you the story of *Gangama*?'

'Not really. All I know is that Ganga flowed from the locks of Shiva.'

'You mean, Lord Shiv*ji* Maharaj,' she said, reminding me to be respectful when referring to gods.

'Alright, alright, Lord Shiva.'

'But that's just one part of a long story. So you don't even know about *Gangama*.'

'Come, Shabnam, tell me the myth about Gangaji.'

'It's not a myth, *bhaijaan*. It's a true story. It happened a long time ago.' I was glad that Shabnam was gradually pulling out of her sentiment of death. Her innocent youth began to glimmer in her eyes, and laying aside the morbid anxieties of her life, she began to recount her childhood memories which, in fact, were no different from my own.

'Long ago, there was a king called Himavat. Ganga was his eldest daughter. She had the unique power of purifying anything that touched her... One day, the *devas*, the gods, led by Brahma, approached the king and asked him to send Ganga to earth so that she could purify all creatures. The king was a bit wary because Ganga was known to be whimsical and unpredictable and, therefore, could well bring harm to the earth. However, since Ganga could also do a lot of good, Himavat agreed.

The earth at that time was completely destroyed by the *asuras*, the demons. Crops uprooted, houses burnt, young children mutilated by the demons, it was dreadful... No-one knew where the demons came from and where they hid. Everyone was in a fix. The *devas* went to Lord Vishnu, who promptly informed them that the demons were hiding beneath the ocean and sage Agastya could alone help in bringing them to the surface...

For years the gods tried in vain to look for sage Agastya. Finally he was traced, meditating by a hut. Agastya was upset to hear about the human woes caused by the demons and offered to drink up the ocean in order to unmask them. He drank up the waters and the *asuras* were revealed.

The *devas* at once pounced on them and killed them without pity. Now the gods asked the great sage to fill up the ocean with water. 'But I've already digested the ocean. How do you expect me to fill it up again?' he said.

The gods now approached Lord Brahma. He could not help.

But Vishnu reassured them, 'Don't panic. King Sagar and his descendants will fill the ocean again.' The *devas* were relieved, but one of them remembered that Sagar had no sons. How could his descendants then...'

'Hey, Shabnam, your story is getting too complicated,' I interrupted her recitation, 'now who was Sagar, Shabnam?'

'Oho!' she exclaimed like a little girl, 'Don't be impatient, don't be impatient. I'm coming to that.'

'Make it simple, Shabnam, I get lost in these long stories.'

'Just be patient. It'll all become clear. Now King Sagar had been doing penance precisely because he had no sons. One day Lord Shiva appeared before him and said, 'I am very pleased with your piety. You shall have 60,000 heroic sons from one wife but they will all die. However, your other wife, Keshini, will bear you one son who will continue your dynasty.' King Sagar was happy. The 60,000 sons grew up to be brave and virtuous.

The other son, Asamanja, the one from Keshini, was wicked. One day, Asamanja drowned a child. The people were angry and so Sagar banished him from his kingdom. However, Asamanja's son, Ansuman, was adored by the people.

One morning, the king was performing the sacred horse sacrifice, *ashwamedha*. The ceremony was about to begin when, suddenly, the King of Gods, Indra, crept in stealthily and stole the sacrificial horse... The horse stolen! *Ashwamedha* sacrifice disrupted! Havoc! What could be worse for a king!

So, Sagar ordered all his 60,000 children to go recover the horse. For years they searched the entire earth but could not find a trace of him. Then they dug a deep tunnel into the earth to search the nether-world. There, they saw a huge elephant, one of the eight who balance the earth on their backs. They moved on, searching high and low. After years they found the ceremonial horse standing beside a meditating sage, Kapila. Excited to find the horse, the princes screamed: 'Thief! Return our horse, you fake sage!' With one stroke, the infuriated sage reduced the 60,000 children to ashes.

The princes did not return. King Sagar got worried until, one night, he recollected what Lord Shiva had told him.'

'What had Lord Shiva said, *bhaijaan*? Do you remember?'

'Who? Shiva? Lord Shiva? What had he said?' Shabnam had caught me sleeping through her story.

'Oho! Remember, Lord Shiva had told Sagar that all his sixty thousand children would die but his lineage would be continued by the single son from the other queen. So Sagar promptly sent out Ansuman to go and look for his uncles. Ansuman reached the nether-world and found the horse standing beside the meditating sage. He saluted the sage and asked him about his uncles. The sage said that he had destroyed them for their impertinent behavior. Ansuman was grieved and wept bitterly. The sage was touched and said: 'There's only one way by which your uncles can now go to heaven. Ganga must be brought down from the celestial world and if her waters can touch your uncles' ashes, they will be purified.'

'Is that why, Shabnam, the Hindus immerse the ashes of their dead in the Ganga?'

'Oho! Yes, of course. Don't tell me you didn't even know that!'

Then pointing her finger towards a little cave, she said:

'You see that tiny dark hole there?'

'Yes, that's some saint's cave.'

'Well, it saved my life yesterday.'

'How?'

'On my way up to Gaumukh yesterday, I was caught in a big storm. That's where I sought shelter and had some food.'

'And where did you spend the night, then?'

'At the *Lal Baba Ashram*.'

'But I slept there too! I didn't see you there.'

'But I didn't go in. I slept in the corridor outside.'

'Silly girl. Why didn't you come in? It's an *ashram* for the pilgrims.'

'Yes, I know, but my father said that I had to do the journey without any comfort. Anyway, to get back to the story... Where was I? Oh yes! So Ansuman was told that Ganga must be brought down from the heavens...

Meanwhile, the stolen horse was retrieved. Ansuman came back and King Sagar managed to complete the horse-sacrifice and save his kingdom from doom. But bringing Ganga down was the biggest problem. King Sagar did penance for his children and died. Ansuman, who succeeded him, did penance and died too. His son, Dilipa, abandoned worldly pleasures and went to the Himalayas and underwent great hardships but he, too, did not succeed in making the Ganga descend. Ultimately when his son, Bhagirath, was meditating in the forest, Lord Brahma appeared before him and asked him for the boon he desired. 'Then, O my Lord,' implored Bhagirath, "let Ganga flow down to earth and deliver the souls of my ancestors." Brahma suddenly turned thoughtful: "I can order Ganga to descend, but the earth cannot sustain the force of her fall. Only Lord Shiva can..."

Now Bhagirath began his penance to Lord Shiva. For one long year, he stood on one leg and chanted prayers until the snake-god appeared before him and agreed to take the force of Ganga on his head. But, said Lord Shiva, "Ganga is unpredictable and destructive. She can cause havoc. So be very careful when you guide her on the earth.'

At long last, Ganga descended. She was wicked, clever, whimsical. Half-way down the heavens, finding Shiva off his guard, she even thought of sweeping him away with her frenzied waters but Lord Shiva saw through her intention, and swung his tresses wide open and tied her into the locks of his long hair. As Ganga lay caught up in Lord Shiva's *jata*, Bhagirath's ancestors were still wailing in hell. Bhagirath pleaded: 'Have pity on my ancestors, Lord, and release Ganga.' So Ganga was at last released. Bhagirath led her over the ocean, down to the nether-world. His fore-fathers' souls were redeemed, the ocean was once again filled with water and Ganga, purified through contact with Lord Shiva's hair, became the source of washing all human sins...'

Shabnam looked up at me with a glint in her eye and, then, clapping her hands, she said: 'That's the story about Bhagirath! That's why Ganga is also called Bhagirathi and the sea, sagar...'

'It is really a beautiful story, Shabnam.'

'Now you know why I came here! Like so many other Hindus, my father sent me here to ask for a boon. Do you know what I asked Ganga*ma* at Gaumukh? I asked her to give half the days remaining to me to *amma* so she can live longer. And you? What did you ask for?'

'Nothing.'

'Nothing?'

'Yes, nothing, Shabnam.'

'But why? Didn't you want something special? There's always a purpose behind such pilgrimages.'

'Not mine. I don't know what to ask for.'

'No, *bhaijaan*, you're not telling me the truth. Tell me, what made you come to Gaumukh? Illness? Some special wish? Children's future? Something!' Shabnam was pleading, almost as if she felt cheated by my reserve.

'Nothing, Shabnam. One fine day, I just picked up my bags and left for Ganga. Must there always be a reason behind each journey?'

'But a pilgrimage to the source of Ganga*ji*, *Bhaijaan*, is not just any other journey.' Shabnam looked far from satisfied with my answer.

'Yes, but then she was Ganga.'
'Who?'
'She.'

Deep in the valley below, Ganga, the river-woman, was serpenting musically on her way to fill the spiritual void of the seas. A million stones, like nuns in white hoods, sat by her banks awaiting answers to questions that made life an eternal enigma. Indifferent, Ganga flowed freely on the wings of human expectancy. Shabnam came close to me and took my hand with affection, little realising that her wonderful myth had struck a painful chord in me. One day, sitting by the Seine, Jaya had said: 'Ganga has the unique gift of uniting the profane and the pure, the erotic and the religious, the *punya* and the *paap*, the good and the evil... I am a sinner Nishant, a *kafir*, an infidel, born in the land of believers.' The red-hot fingers of this myth had enkindled a fire in that secret space of my *being* which I had left behind with my childhood. A strange existentialist nothingness clasped me from within. Deep inside I felt a tinge of cruelty and callousness, a state of mind, whose first victim is the sentiment for real life. I knew that we were approaching Gangotri and, soon, Shabnam would make her painful way along pathways which led to a merciless death and, yet, I could offer this innocent angel nothing but the mask of a comforting illusion. She must have sensed my mood, for she asked: '*Bhaijaan*, you'll escort me to Lanka, won't you?' She sought from me confidence, precisely when I sought distance.

'To Lanka?'
'It's not far, *bhaijaan*.'
'But that's not the point, Shabnam. Your father has asked you to do the journey alone.'
'But I need you, *bhaijaan*,' she said, clutching my hand.
'Pilgrimage is penance, Shabnam. Emotion has no place in penance.'

'*Chaliye, chaliye,* come, *bhaijaan.*'
'No, Shabnam, I can't.'
'What's come over you? Come.'
'I can't.'
'Why?'
'Didn't your mother tell you the story of Shantanu and Ganga?' I asked her.
'What's the story?'
'When Shantanu begged Ganga to stay back and not leave him alone... Ganga looked at him with piteous eyes and declared: "I shall not come back. When the sun has set on a day, it is foolish to ask him to come back so that you can live the day once again. The sun once set shall never return to the same day."'
'I don't understand all this, *bhaijaan?* Come, I need you, I am lonely. Show me the way.'
'I'm sorry, Shabnam, I cannot. You had come to seek from Ganga*ma* a lease of life for your ailing mother. I pray she grants you the boon. But I have nothing to seek from her. I came here because I had loved her reincarnation. And I must remain here to live the pain of a love which you cannot have and which you cannot leave. The sun has set, Shabnam. We cannot have it again. We are condemned to live the pain of its disappearance and reappearance.'

We parted. From a distance, I saw Shabnam, her arm folded over her face, leaning against a rock. The wind carried the sound of her naked chagrin. Soaked in tears, back to the cries of the umbilical cord, she was the tragic essence of any pilgrimage. Right below her, the Gangotri temple stood as ever before, in divine indifference, least affected by the emotions of a parched earth. It is when you need gods the most that they seem to exist the least.

Pahar

ALL DEPARTURES OR SEPARATIONS LEAVE BEHIND A similar pain. The same hollow, the same gentle rain within, the same foetus suspended on the horizon. Separation offers a glimpse of finitude, of the end of union; it restirs the awareness that a human being, at various stages of his life, is basically the changing form of the same, lonely foetus. In a world where nothing is, where everything must be transient and ephemeral, separation reiterates that we are alone, all alone, under the gaze of a million eyes. Separation, therefore, is nothing but a man before his foetal mirror, and if Shabnam and I felt the pain of parting, it was only because we recognized ourselves once again in the same mirror.

Bahadur, the caretaker at the Gangotri rest house, woke me up in the morning with a steaming cup of tea. Putting a bucket of water in the bathroom, he said: 'I'm sorry, *sahib*, the bathroom mirror broke yesterday. I'm afraid you'll have to shave without one.' In a world of countless illusions, it certainly did not worry me that yet another mirror had broken. 'I hope the water is hot, Bahadur. I was thinking of having a good wash before leaving.' Feeling the water with his hand, Bahadur assured, 'Yes, *sahib*. It is very hot. Your shoes are drying by the fire and breakfast should be ready in a few minutes. The porter has also arrived. I've settled him for a hundred rupees up to Lanka.'

Mohan Singh, the new porter, was another immigrant from

Nepal. At the beginning he seemed a bit reserved, as if trying to gauge my temperament, but once he discovered that he was in the company of someone who also enjoyed good conversation, Mohan revealed his true self. Boisterous and amicably blunt, Mohan Singh did not hesitate to make full use of his colourful tongue. Lifting my bag with a quick, jerky movement, he asked:

'Is this all you are travelling with?'

'Well, I am not on an expedition, Mohan.'

'But this bag is too light, *sahib*,' he retorted, a cheeky look in his eyes.

'You call that light! It blew the daylights out of me the other day!'

'O no, *sahib*. This is nothing. A *Pahari* porter must have at least fifty kilos on his head, or he runs the risk of flying off into the air. *Sahib*, if only I could tell you stories about the *Paharis* and the mules...'

Mohan tossed my bag high up in the air and caught it again with a touch of arrogant ease. Turning towards me, he asked:

'But if you are not a *tirekker sahib*, why did you come think of coming up here in the winter?'

'Winters are beautiful, aren't they?'

'Are you a pilgrim?'

'Well, who isn't in this life?'

'But where are you going, *sahib*?' Mohan asked, intrigued.

'Lanka.'

'And then?'

'Down the Himalayas.'

'But there are no buses these days, *sahib*.'

'I know. There's a jeep waiting for me at Lanka. I had asked my driver to look out for me this morning.'

'And then? Where will you go after that?'

'Don't know. Wherever Ganga takes me...'

'But Ganga will take you on paths where your jeep can't go, *sahib*.'

'Maybe I won't go by jeep then.'

'Will you go on a boat, *sahib*? How exciting!'

'Maybe.'

'And why are you going down Ganga, *sahib*?'

'If only I knew...'

Reacting impatiently to my errant mysticism, Mohan suddenly lunged at a wild plant and plucked a leaf from it. 'Do you know this leaf, *sahib*? It's excellent for black dysentery.' Mohan was so full of life that he could hardly walk straight down the path. He serpented ceaselessly between the two edges of the track, looking curiously around, here a bird, there a butterfly, plucking leaves or stroking tree-trunks. Mohan also had a keen eye for the wild fruit in the region, making me taste some ten different fruits, flowers or wild vegetables. At one point he asked me to wait, went down the mountain and came back with a roll of some transparent substance which resembled parchment. Handing it over to me, he said: 'Here, *sahib*, a little souvenir from the Garhwal Himalayas. This is *bhojpata*, the bark of a tree on which our scriptures were once written.' Restless as ever, Mohan stopped again after a few minutes and remarked:

'Only foreigners have such bags. How did you get one?'

'Well, I live abroad.'

'But you speak Hindi!'

'Why not? It's my mother tongue.'

'Ah! I see. I was a bit confused this morning. Your clothes and your manner seemed quite foreign but you spoke Hindi. So I couldn't really place you. Tell me, *sahib*, what do you think about the *goras*, the white people?'

'Well, it depends on who you're talking about.'

'I find them very funny.'

'Do you know many foreigners?'

'Well, you know, I've worked as a porter for many tourists.'

'In Nepal?'

'No, over here in Garhwal. They're very strange people, *sahib*.'

'Why, did someone walk away without paying you?'

'On the contrary, they pay rather well. But, *sahib*, they're a very shameless breed.'

'Did someone offend you, Mohan?'

'No, *sahib*. But I was just thinking about the way they conduct themselves in life. They kiss and embrace in the open. They make love where they please.'

'Where did you peep in, Mohan, that you saw them make love!'

'Oh *sahib*, not once, many times. We porters see it all the time when working for the tourist *tirekkers*. There was a couple once who made love round-the-clock. The whole night, the woman was screaming and squeaking in the tent. Another day, the same couple started their business on the bus and the conductor had to stop them in the middle of all the fireworks! Then, the other day, a foreign girl got fond of a porter and virtually jumped on him during a night-halt. The man was shocked. He begged her, "Madam, leave me alone. Madam, I'm just a poor porter. I'm your servant." But the woman forced him. Later, by the time the story got around, the woman had left, but the poor Nepalese porter lost his job. No, *sahib*, we find them quite a loose people.'

'Come on, Mohan, stop being prudish. People in the hills make love in the open too.'

'But not in the same way. Our women don't scream and squirm like this. Our women are decent. No. They're a funny lot, *sahib*.' Mohan reflected for a while and, then, asked me: 'Are you married, *sahib*?'

'No. Are you?'

'Yes, *sahib*, she's just come and joined me after fifteen years of marriage…'

Mohan Singh left home at ten. His family, with one cow as their sole means of livelihood, did not have enough food and so Mohan, like his elder brother before him, was sent to India in search of money. His first job was as a tea-boy, earning twenty rupees a month. Like any other child of his age, Mohan had his own fancies and fits of revolt against the world of discipline and drudgery. He changed jobs frequently. Carrying headloads, boot-polishing, grazing cattle, fruit-picking, domestic help, road works–he experienced them all. Sleeping out in the streets and municipal parks, beaten and roughed up by local toughs and bribe-fleecing cops, Mohan's world was the world of the downtrodden. All he wished was to save enough to be able to make a short trip back home to see his mother.

'I saw mothers with their young children in the bazaar, and it made me cry to think of my mother.' After eight or ten years he had enough in his pocket to buy the fare. On his arrival, he learnt that his mother had passed away and that his fifty-year-old father was lying on his death-bed. The father insisted on seeing Mohan married before he died. Mohan got married, winning a cow in his dowry. Two days after his wedding, his brother wrote from India, asking him to hurry back since there was promise of a better job. Without even having felt the face of his wife properly, Mohan left for India. On the heels of his departure, his father died…

Mohan could not write nor his wife read. There was virtually no communication between the two, except for a few insipid letters, business-like missives written by a literate intermediary at work. On returning from Nepal, Mohan found his new job slightly better and he managed to save eight hundred rupees over the next three years. He thought of investing his savings to learn some technical skill. One fine evening, his savings in his pocket, he left for Rishikesh, a town in the foothills of the Himalayas, where an old hometown acquaintance had promised to take him on as a car workshop apprentice. *En route*, he got robbed and beaten up. He was back to square one. Like the proverbial spider on the palm tree, the eternal cycle of life began again.

'Mohan, take it easy, take it easy, I can't run like you.' His pace was unrelenting for my nicotine-stained lungs.

'Would you like to take a breather, *sahib*?' he asked.

'If you don't mind.'

I sat on a tiny bridge constructed by the Indian Army, while Mohan got busy with his favourite pastime of picking leaves and petals of wild plants. Then, as if fed up with his own habit of nibbling at any odd leaf, Mohan took out a little box from his pocket containing powdered tobacco and limestone. Looking up towards me, he said:

'You smoke cigarettes, don't you? People who smoke cigarettes don't care for *tambakoo-choona*. Like to try some?'

'Are you sure it's just that?'

'What else, *sahib*?'

'*Zarda*, opium, could be anything. I don't trust you, Mohan.' I said in jest.

'No, no. I have none of those vices.'

'Fine. I don't mind trying some'. Taking a couple of pinches of tobacco and limestone powder, I said to Mohan,

'So you've had a tough life, haven't you?'

'But the story is not over yet. Ten or fifteen years after my marriage, I got a good job. A man from my village helped me find a job in the Forest Department. If all went well, I was told, I would soon become a permanent government employee, and you know that government jobs are quite good. For the first time I had a roof over my head. My boss gave me a servant's quarter in his house.'

'And your wife?'

'Well, of course, I sent her my very first salary and she came to live with me.' Mohan burst out laughing. 'You know what? We didn't recognize each other at the railway station! Anyway the fellow who had got me the job was involved with the *Chipko* movement.'

'You mean the same *Chipko* where the people in the hills prevented government contractors from chopping down the trees?'

'Yes, you're right. The same lot. I got involved with the movement. Being born and brought up in the mountains, naturally I sympathized with the cause. I hate the contractors who come from the plains, chop down trees, play havoc with our lives. They have no respect for the hills. They're merely interested in the loot. Then, *sahib*, felling trees does not only mean losing a forest but a thousand other things as well. The contractors wouldn't let our women pick firewood or graze cattle. Then, deforestation makes the soil infirm. That causes landslides and landslides block rivers and cause floods. And when flood-waters break through the sand, they sweep away houses, cattle, villages, everything. A thousand effects, *sahib*. Then, the contractors bring in bad city habits. Corruption, bribes, infighting—our entire lives get upset. So, to keep the devils out, I joined the Chipko movement. Demonstrations, putting up posters, attending meetings...'

'But Mohan, were you by now a permanent employee with the Forest Department, or were you still on probation?'

'Yes, *sahib*, that's exactly the point. I was still a temporary worker. Now my boss got to find out that I was involved with the movement. He tried to interrogate me a couple of times but couldn't get much information out of me. Then, one fine morning, someone knocked at my door. I opened it, and it was the police...'

'For being involved with the Chipko?'

'No, no. They said that my boss had filed a complaint that I had stolen a gold necklace from his house. I didn't have a clue to the theft. I could swear on my wife, on God, on Ganga*ma*, on anyone. It was a complete frame-up. I was taken to the police station, beaten up for a month and then released. On my return, I lost my job, my quarters and was asked to leave. Some political friends said they would fight my case, but I was not interested. I gave up the whole thing, and came and settled in the mountains. We have a cow at home. My wife sells milk, I am a porter.' After a brief silence, Mohan added, 'This is all *karma, sahib*. Do you believe in God?'

Mohan Singh, like millions in the country, was remarkable for the cold and indifferent manner in which he recounted a tragic autobiography. Having become insular to the world of human sentiments, he had no conception of sorrow or tragedy. The fitful drama of his life was taken as something inscribed in the very nature of his proletarian birth, and what was tragedy for me, was for him yet another absurd detail of a long and listless life. Neither the caprice of *karma* nor the concepts of modern rationality could explain the intricacies of his thought-process. In his day to day life, he was aware that it was the rich, the politicians and the crooks who made the laws of history, and that the jails of his penuried *karma* stemmed from the vile machinations of the fat and ugly employer. But Mohan also knew that the only way to find harmony in this merciless bazaar of commodities was to reluctantly submit to a preordained destiny which the invisible gods had, avowedly, bestowed on his life. It was this dual tension, between a passive fatalism and a historical consciousness, which provided the first explanation to the mind of a wage-earner not fully absorbed by the structures of modernisation, and yet not completely free from the grip of ancient beliefs and rituals. 'When reality is cruel,' Mohan mused, 'then let life be a dream.'

We reached Lanka by noon. Mihir Singh, the jeep-driver, was nowhere to be seen. The whole place looked deserted. The snowfall of the past few days seemed to have chased all birds, animals and men indoors. Mohan climbed up to the top of the hill and shouted, 'Mihir, Mihir Singh.' His voice echoed in the mountains, but there was no response. Finding his voice fall on deaf ears, he yelled out one last time: 'Are you asleep, you fat slobs! Are you going to spend the whole day with your wives?' An incomprehensible reply floated our way. We crossed the bridge and walked over to the village.

Much to my surprise, the word had spread fast and no sooner had I stepped into the village than Mihir Singh came rushing towards me and announced nervously:

'*Sahib, sahib,* the jeep has frozen. It's like a slab of ice.'

'What happened? It's not all that cold. It should work on choke.'

'Oh *sahib*! The diesel, the water, everything is frozen like ice. I've been trying to start it all morning, but it just won't start.'

Mihir led me to the jeep and flung its hood open. As I bent over the radiator to check if the carburettor-points were properly connected, I noticed a little *kangri*, a pot of glowing red-hot charcoal, placed ingeniously by the distributor. 'But this will make the whole thing explode!' I exclaimed, horrified at the sight of flames in an engine. 'No, no, *sahib*, no problem. This is nothing. Earlier on, I had lit a big fire under the engine. When I ran out of dry wood, I had no option but to use a small *kangri*.' Not quite convinced by his dangerous solutions, I asked Mihir to put out the fire but he insisted that there was no danger and, if anything, he needed some more dry wood to heat the jeep quickly. Mihir added, smilingly: 'Don't worry, *sahib*. Fire is harmless, it is the most sacred deity in my region.'

Since I knew nothing about automobile mechanics, I let Mihir dabble in his anachronistic thermo-therapy. Mohan, who seemed to know virtually everyone in the village, managed to procure some dry sticks and Mihir lost no time in lighting two big fires under the jeep. Mihir heated the jeep for about fifteen minutes—like chicken in the rotisserie oven—and then asked Mohan to round up people who could help push the jeep. A whistle from Mohan's mouth was enough for dozens of people and screaming children to come running down to surround the fresh-roasted body of a Mahindra jeep. The heat-therapy was pulled out. I took the wheel and Mohan orchestrated the push. Half-an-hour of muscle-flexing and the jeep stirred nervously, jerking, jolting, bouncing and bumping, releasing balls of hot air reminiscent of five-star hotel gastric disorders. The roar of the engine provoked such stupendous excitement that it seemed as if the cheering men, women and children were applauding the successful launching of the first vehicle made on earth.

It was well past noon and the weather was fast deteriorating. Rishikesh, our next halt, was a seven-hour non-stop run from Lanka, and with a jeep which ran less on automobile mechanics than on the vagaries of its own humour, there was every reason to try and leave as early as possible. Mihir and Mohan dumped my bag and their bedding-rolls into the jeep, and we were all set to leave. Just then, a group of villagers came up to us and enquired whether we were going up to Tehri. Mihir did not even have the chance to react when several village elders, completely impervious to our hesitation, climbed into the jeep one by one. By the time I had counted the last head, there were ten of them packed in the back. While Mihir fretted and fumed, an old man blurted angrily: 'Stop it, you fusspot! If you insist we'll pay you an extra rupee per head...'

The descent to Uttarkashi was slow. The weight of thirteen passengers had reduced the braking-power of the jeep so drastically, that at every sharp turn or slope, we were compelled to drive at a crawling pace. Things, however, improved after Uttarkashi. Five passengers decided to get off, probably more out of fear of paying that extra rupee than out of sympathy for the poor jeep. If the vehicle felt lighter after Uttarkashi, the weather made matters worse than before. A heavy downpour, accompanied by strong, chilly winds, caused the mercury to drop by a good ten degrees, and frequent landslides made driving tense and dangerous. We were not far from Tehri, when I asked my companions:

'How about a cup of tea somewhere?'

'What a wonderful idea!' shouted Mohan from the back, 'There's a tea-stall a few miles down the road.'

'I hope the place is clean, Mohan,' queried Mihir, with the suspicion of a new urbanite looking down upon his rural past.

'That depends on what you pay! Give them good money, you'll get good tea and pure milk. Give them twenty-five paise a cup, you'll get horse piss!'

Ten kilometres short of Tehri, we pulled up at a cluster of ramshackle tea-stalls. The very sight of a hot oven and spiralling clouds of smoke and steam were enough to warm our chilled bodies and dampening spirits. A group of people huddled around the mud-oven were busy talking in feverish excitement.

We walked down to one of the tea-shops, and Mohan promptly ordered six special *chais,* insisting that each cup contain at least one *chatank* of pure milk. Just as we had taken our positions around the fire, a stranger walked towards us.

'I knew it. I knew it,' he muttered to himself, 'The village astrologer had predicted it a long time ago. He had said clearly that India was passing through a bad period, that the planet *Shani* augured great calamities for the country.' Suddenly turning towards me, he asked:

'How many do they say have died?'

'Died? Where?' I was perplexed.

'How many have died in the explosion?'

'What explosion?'

'They've just arrived here,' explained the tea-stall owner. 'Perhaps you don't know that an atom bomb has exploded in India.'

'What? An atom bomb?'

'Yes, an atom bomb!'

Was I hallucinating? 'Do you know what an atom bomb is?'

'Come on, *sahib*, stop treating us like idiots. An atom bomb has exploded. The gas has already killed 5000 people.'

'Where? In Iran? Iraq? Lebanon? What are you saying? Where?' I must confess that I must have sounded a bit hysterical.

'I told you, didn't I? Atom bomb in India. In Bhopal.'

'Where did you hear that? Do you have a radio here?'

'No, we don't have a radio. A man just told us about it. It was in the papers. We all saw it. There was even a photograph showing how a man had got blinded by the gas.'

'But what are you saying?' I asked, eager for some more precise information. 'And when did the explosion take place?'

'Yesterday. At eleven in the morning.'

'Are you sure it was an atom bomb?'

'Yes, yes, *sahib*. Dead certain. Let me tell you what happened. The man informed us that a bomb had exploded in the city of Bhopal. Virtually the whole city of Bhopal has been wiped out. The gas has killed thousands and thousands of people. Cattle, men, women, children, young, old... There was another photograph which showed people running all over the place.'

'Are you sure you read it was an atomic explosion?'

'Well, I may not have been to college, but I think that's what we read.'

'You think or did you read it with your own eyes?'

'Don't believe me if you don't want to,' he retorted angrily, 'ask someone else.'

While I was busy trying to figure out what really must have happened, the tea-stall conversation turned into a riveting thriller. Gripped with excitement, full of certitude, people discussed among themselves with the lucidity of a science-fiction writer.

'I tell you this is Pakistan's doing,' said one.

'We've been hearing about Pakistan making a bomb for a long time now,' said another, before having second thoughts: 'Though it could also be China. They've had a bomb for centuries.'

'Rubbish! Centuries!' refuted yet another, 'The atom bomb is only about ten years old.'

'Yes, yes, he's quite right. It could be China, and it's so close by. Beyond Gaumukh, it's all China. But it's strange, isn't it? We didn't notice any planes fly past yesterday.'

'I saw a helicopter. But it was going the other way–towards Gangotri.'

'No, no,' said the man who had begun the discussion, 'it's got to be Pakistan. They've been scheming ever since we gave them a good thrashing in the 1971 war. I'm sure it's them. But tell me, how much did the man say the bomb weighs?'

'Ten thousand tons.'

'*Hareram, hareram, hareram!* With that sort of a weight, you don't need any gases. It can kill everyone by its sheer weight!'

Just then, a haggard-looking *Pahari*, his clothes drenched in rain, walked in for a cup of tea. He was immediately informed about the national calamity.

'Eh Ramlal, have you heard this? They've dropped an atom

bomb on Bhopal!'

'It must have been the Sikh terrorists! Indira's head was not enough, so they dropped a bomb on Delhi.'

'But who said Delhi was bombed?'

'Of course, the planes first bombed Delhi, then moved towards Bhopal.'

'Really? Delhi bombed?'

'Yes.'

'Good God! Rajiv Gandhi must also have died, too'

'Relax, young boys!' advised the old man, 'What are you getting excited about? So long as Garhwal is safe, live in peace!'

The young *Paharis* were still busy discussing the nuclear explosion when Mihir noticed that the Dehradun-Uttarkashi bus, going uphill, had just arrived. He rushed to the bus and asked an educated-looking man:

'Is it true that there has been an atomic explosion in Delhi?'

'Not that I've heard of.'

'They say Bhopal was also bombed?'

'Not bombed. The morning papers said there was a lethal gas-leak in Bhopal. Thousands have died.'

'And Rajiv?' asked Mihir, 'Is he dead too?'

'No, who said that?'

'They say Rajiv has died?'

'Don't worry! People in that family don't die until the next generation is ready to take over...'

Desire

RISHIKESH WAS FAST ASLEEP. THE PILGRIMS SNORED, the priests dozed, the temple witnessed its own cremation pyre. A distant flag fluttered lazily, its shadow slicing the face of a shivering beggar. It was night, the hour of poetry or crime, the hour of whispered love-makings. Night is the only time when the sun, the moon, the entire cosmos obeys unerringly the dictates of my pagan desire.

I was sitting on the Laxman Jhoola, a toy-like bridge of ropes and wooden planks which Laxman, Lord Rama's brother, had raised to link the severed destiny of Ganga. Feet suspended from the bridge, rocking on the *jhoola*, swept by the heady breeze of a *Rishikeshian* night, I watched the adolescent Ganga emerge from the feet of the sphinx-Himalayas. Uncoiling herself like a serpent, pulling the long black rectangular veil from beneath the gigantic mountain, Ganga woke from the bed of night, much like Jaya arose from the pleasures of an adulterous night.

She woke early, well before dawn, to see the morning rise over leaves, birds and sound. Just as she offered her savannah body at night, she greeted the dawn with the deep reverence of an erotic believer. She had a unique art of offering. With measured gestures, well-chosen words, everything balanced and proportioned, she greeted the morning so as not to disturb the natural grace of a creeping light. As I still lay, nestling in the warmth of her odours, she, like a true Brahmin, hurried to her morning shower, and bathing, hummed a Kannada melody, whose sound is the most precious memory that I could offer to the waking Ganga. She showered long, till the water in the pipes ran cold. Often I would wake with Jaya still under the shower, giggling like a child: 'Oh! The water is ice cold.' Dressed and clean, perfumed with *khas-itr*, she would then light incense, carrying its fragrance all over the house lest any part be left impure. Finishing the act of showing respect to her gods, she would then watch the sunlight crawl down the walls until it was time to whisper in my ear: 'Get up, sweetheart, see the Clementine is aglow.'

On the way down from Rishikesh, I debated stopping over at my uncle's who lived on the outskirts of the town. There was no real purpose in visiting him apart from the fact that I had given his address as one of the few places where I could be contacted. Several weeks had passed since Jaya had left but, no matter how great the despair in love, there comes a day when a faint hope within you says, 'There may be a letter from her.' My uncle was on his way to work. Surprised to see my jeep at his doorstep, he exclaimed:

'Nishant! You? What are you doing here?'

'I just thought I'd stop by and say hello.'

'But what brings you to these parts of the world?'

'Oh! I am on work.'

'What work? Writing on French hippies for your newspaper, are you?'

'No, no. Hippies are long forgotten. I'm going down Ganga in a boat.'

'You mean you've become a hippie yourself!' he remarked mockingly. 'What's this business of Ganga? Going down the entire length of Ganga?'

'Well, yes.'

'And you call that work! Strange! The most sacred pilgrimage for a Hindu is to your newspaper an exotic reportage. Don't these newspapers abroad have anything better to write about?'

'Come off it, uncle. This is not for a newspaper.'

'Don't tell me that you've become a Hindu believer!' he said, cynically.

'No. But tell me, is there any mail for me?'

'Male? Mail? What mail? You mean a letter.'

'Yes.'

'No. I don't think so. Not that I can recall anyway.'

'Nothing? Are you sure.'

'Well, on second thoughts, I think there was a parcel for you. Let me take a look. It should be somewhere on the table.'

For one long hour he plodded through heaps and heaps of paper, and each time he failed to find it, muttered: 'It wasn't anything important. It was in a yellowish envelope. It looked like some publicity material. You know the kind of material that the Bible Society of India keeps sending. It didn't look important at all and that's why I must have misplaced it.'

Finally, after a long search, he found the parcel. It was a manuscript from my brother, Jugnu, my literary god-father. Ironically, his new book was called *Mera Khat*, My Letter. I flipped through the first few pages. Marvellous writing, but like his writings before, it was filled with expressionist pain and sorrow. I packed the manuscript in my bag and thought of writing to Jaya.

jaya,

> *the autumn came with you. it disappeared with you. it disappeared in you. you remain, as ever before, the lone confidante to whom she shall disclose the secret of her mysterious osmosis.*
>
> *since you left, seasons have changed over the surface of snow, light and wind, and time has described an arch of distance*

which joins as much as it un-joins, the bond of a real autumn to an imaginary spring. if anything has remained unaltered, it is the splash of pomegranate in parc montsouris by whose windswept leaves your hair passes into the pages of a sublime history.

the sun shines weepingly. the transparent curtain is obliquely drawn. over its edge, i see a tree in the garden below, its leaves, autumnally yellow, are wafting to a memory already a few months old.

its bacchic branches
dark and tanned
like the scorching embrace of your nightly arms
whistle through the arterial frame of your matchless dreams.

what is absence, jaya? the bathroom gets wet, i think of you. tea spills on the bed, i think of you. a cat is struck, i think of you. ganga smiles, i think of you.

i want to die on the sun-dial of time.

i am on the ganga descending from her mysterious source. i have just reached rishikesh where she assumes the form of that mythical serpent that the hindus have worshipped through history. soon, on it, my lonesome boat shall be heaven-bound with the eternal riddle: who am i? who is she? why is she here and yet not here? why has she gone and yet not gone? where is the laxman jhoola, the bridge over two desires? if only i could flow like ganga into the bosom of the infinite seas...

i haven't written all these days.

to write is to resurface the traumatic subterraneanity of mind.

it is to feel the real, more real than the real. writing is an unguided descent into those unknown regions of the self where you, per chance, touched me. to write is to meet solitude, face to face, just the way we meet on wet sand in a moment of infinite pleasures. nothing is more creative than a solitude where the presence of the other, your presence, is more present than ever. if only i could peel you a Clementine...

> *imagination sits longing*
> *on the threshold of unbelievable absences*
> *on doorsteps of ambiguous void*
> *on the keyhole of murderous perceptions*
> *you are the sweetness of an endless autumn, jaya*
> *a strange season inscribed on the destiny of man*
> *you are the miracle by which leaves change colours*
> *the magic by which ganga wears her sparrow-veil*
> *life is a carnival where marriages join funerals...*

nishant

There was a long queue at the post office. The Bhopal gas tragedy was on everyone's lips. While most of them denounced the government, a Congress Party sympathizer even insinuated that the gas-leak was nothing but an opposition ploy to unseat the government in the coming elections. It was a good half-an-hour's wait in the queue before my turn finally came.

'May I have some stamps for this envelope, please?'

'Yes, yes. Of course, yes. Where is the letter going, *sahib*?'

The man sounded unusually polite for an Indian post office.

'To Pakistan.'

'Where? To Pakistan? You said Pakistan, did you?'

'Yes, to Pakistan.'

He looked at me suspiciously.

'What's in the envelope?' he asked.

'Just a letter. Why? Since when have we started banning mail to Pakistan?'

'No, no, there are no bans. You see, brother, you can send letters wherever you like, but we have to be a bit careful of our enemies. Especially these days... The French are spying in India, the Poles are spying, American companies are leaking gases to kill our people. And, now, Pakistan is training the Sikh terrorists!'

'Please... I'm in a hurry. How much does it cost for Pakistan please?'

'How do I know?' he quipped. 'How much does the envelope weigh?'

'How would I know?' I retorted. 'Please weigh it for me.'

'This is not the weighing counter. Have it weighed at Counter No. 5.'

He shoved my envelope away with his hand, and said 'Next!'

'Excuse me, sir, I'm in a hurry. It would be very kind of you to weigh it at your counter.'

'Please make room for the next person, mister. Everyone is in a hurry these days. People behind you are also in a rush. Come on, please move on. Yes, please, next.'

It took me another twenty minutes to reach the man at Counter No. 5.

'Could you please weigh this letter for me? It's for Pakistan.'

'Pakistan or America, Dubai or Saudi Arabia, Honolulu or Timbuktoo, my job is to weigh. Why should I bother about destinations?' He weighed the letter in his hand and mused:

'Should be about ten grams. I suppose you would need the exact weight.'

'Yes, could you please weigh it for me?'

'I'm very sorry, *sahib*, I don't have the ten-gram weight. I haven't been able to lay my hands on it for three days now.' He searched disinterestedly in his drawer for the weight and then, looking apologetically at me, said:

'Can I ask you for a favour, *sahib*?'

'Yes.'

'Would you mind getting it weighed at the grocery-store

next door? He has all the weights and will do it for you without any problems.'

Avoiding any further argument, I left the post office and went to the shop next door. Two plump *paan*-chewing shopkeepers sat cross-legged, enveloped in the odour of colourful spices.

'Would you weigh this envelope for me, please?' I requested.

'Oh! Oh! Impossible!' the man screamed in anger, 'you mean that bloody post office clerk has still not found his ten gram weight!'

'God help our country!' added the other shopkeeper, 'what's to become of our land! The post office*wala* has obviously sold the weight-box! *Hare Ram!* The government is eaten up by its own men!'

The envelope, which by now resembled a piece of used face-tissue, weighed eleven grams. Before I could hurry back to the post office, the shopkeeper shot me a word of precious advice: 'Be careful, my son. Make sure you see him cross out the stamps on the envelope properly. Otherwise these swines are quite capable of peeling the stamps off and reselling them as new. Dirty world, brother. It's a dirty world!'

My next destination was Hardwar, one of the seven holy pilgrim-sites in India. It is in this city at Hari Ki Pairi that Vishnu left behind his indelible footprint on the banks of Ganga and it is again, in Hardwar, the 'gateway to God', that the myth of Ganga's unique capacity to confer the boon of heaven upon the ashes of the dead translates itself into reality. Each year, millions and millions of pilgrims, bereavement writ large on their faces, descend on the city to immerse the ashes of their dead, hoping that Ganga shall carry in her bosom the sins of the departed to the serene kingdom of the heavens. While the dead receive their boon from the magic touch of the Gangetic waters, the evening prayer, the Hardwar *aarti*, confers peace and solace on those left behind to mourn the memory of their dead.

At Hardwar, Mihir got off the jeep to try and book a room at the Inspection Bungalow, while I drove straight to Hari Ki Pairi for the *aarti*. Thousands of pilgrims stood facing the Ganga temple which resembled a white mushroom floating nervously on the surface of the river. I was making my way through the crowd when suddenly a hundred gongs, descending from the heavens, shook the atmosphere. Executed with rare theatrical precision, their sound cast a spell on the city. The gongs made the temple rock, the windows clatter and the idols smile. An alert or a sonorous signal to announce the arrival of gods on a thirsty earth, the gongs captured, in the fugitive moment of a spell-bound clock, the entire force of a living Hinduism which atheists like me had long consigned to the realm of the dead.

Taking their cue from the gongs, the pilgrims set afloat hundreds of oil-lamps on Ganga, transforming the goddess into a river of light. As the goddess flowed beneath a million flames of desire, the priests lit the silver torches. Within seconds, tufts of fragrant smoke and eleven serpentine flames, some five metres high, wove around Hardwar the reassuring illusion that all the dead would reach the kingdom of heaven, and that peace and prosperity would be the lot of every believer on earth. The chanting, the fragrance, the wind and the light thus created the most hypnotising carnival of dubious beliefs that I had ever witnessed in my life. An absolute hypnosis prevailed. Each appeared pure to the other, as to himself. Each looked divine. Evil seemed dead and yet, strangely, these were the same pilgrims who made possible this planet of deceit, greed and hypocrisy.

Despite my sceptical eye, the *aarti* had on me the effect that camphor has on the body of the sick. The Hardwar prayer creates a unique silence within the mind from which each can draw whatever one is capable of drawing. Some search bodily comfort; others, material prosperity. For me, the *aarti* was that moment of quiet in which the entire mystique of Ganga rose before my eyes. For a few minutes, vast stretches of space and water floated on my retina. I saw Ganga as a little boat lost in the infinitude of her waters, I saw Ganga as the song of a lonely nightingale, I saw Ganga as Jaya, dressed in her best silk, walking majestically out of the pleasures of an amorous night. The daydreams of Ganga were, in fact, not just an optical illusion, for if Mihir's optimism were to be believed, it was the following morning, the day of the inauspicious planet *Shani*, that my boat was to at last embrace the holy surface of Ganga.

As I walked out of Hari Ki Pairi, Mihir greeted me with a smile. 'I was right, *sahib*. The room is booked and the man on duty has sent someone to book the boat for tomorrow. He just took twenty rupees, *sahib*.' Since the journey was to begin early next morning, we drove straight to the bungalow. An immense structure, the inspection bungalow offered a rare insight into the colonial mind: love of open spaces away from a claustrophobic London, taste for the evening tea on the breezy verandas, soft, green walks to contemplate the magic of Ganga, high roofs to evade the scorching heat and large ottomans to recline on and plot strategies for the future of an uneasy colony. The man who looked after reservations was kind, and kinder still, after Mihir managed to slip into his pocket a ten rupee note. Unlocking a palatial suite, the attendant muttered:

'Come in, come in, *sahib*. This is the room where Pandit Jawaharlal Nehru*ji* used to stay.' On the wall were the famous lines:

'The Ganga, especially, is the river of India, beloved of her people, round which are intertwined her racial memories, her hopes and fears, her songs of triumph, her victories and her defeats. She has been a symbol of India's age-long culture and civilization, ever-changing, ever-flowing and ever the same Ganga. She reminds me of the snow-covered peaks and the deep valleys of the Himalayas, which I have loved so much, and of the rich and vast plains below, where my life and work have been cast. Smiling and dancing in the morning sunlight, and dark and gloomy and full of mystery as the evening shadows fall; a narrow, slow and graceful stream in winter, and a vast roaring thing during the monsoon, broad-bosomed almost as the sea, and with something of the sea's power to destroy, the Ganga has been to me a symbol and a memory of the past of India, running into the present, and flowing on to the great ocean of the future.'

We woke up early. A quick cup of tea, a cigarette and we were off to Neel Dhara, the current of Ganga beyond a canal where a rendezvous had been fixed with some boatmen. While I had been at the *aarti* the previous day, Mihir had shopped for the sundry provisions that we would need on the boat-journey. If there were things that we had overlooked, we thought, it would be best to buy them after our meeting with the boatmen who, after all, knew life on the water much better than us. Dawn had still not broken over Hardwar, and the pilgrims were getting ready for the first sacred dip in Ganga. By the time we reached Neel Dhara, the light was distinctly better and Mihir parked the jeep by a bridge. 'It was somewhere around here that I met them yesterday,' he murmured. I descended towards a cluster of ragged structures which could well have been the boatmen's huts. Two men, mashing stalks of *neem* tree between their teeth, squatted on the edge of a boat. Another man, the first to notice my presence, had not yet finished his morning ablutions. Seeing me, he quickly turned his half-bare back to me and started vigorously washing his buttocks with the holy waters. For a moment, I wondered who purifies whom: Gang*ama* him or he Gang*ama*...

'*Jai Ram ji ki*,' I greeted them.

'*Jai Gange, jai Gange, jai Gange*. We've been waiting for you. Are you the one who wanted to rent a boat?'

'Yes, yes. Rather cold today, isn't it?'

'Cold, hot, windy, rainy, stormy, this is all the magic of Ganga*ji*,' they sounded rather exuberant for the early hour. 'But she gives us the strength to bear it all. The weather doesn't bother us. We are born and brought up by these holy waters. She is our mother!'

'Did the man explain my journey to you?' I asked.

'Yes, he came last night. He said that a *sahib* would come to rent a boat. We're ready. Waiting for your orders.'

'Have you packed your bags and everything? It's a long journey.'

'Oh! Don't worry about us, *sahib*, we do such journeys every day. How long would you like to rent the boat for?'

'I don't know. How long will it take?'

'*Sahib*, how can a poor man like me tell you how long it will take? We're here at your service. You are the master. One hour, two hours, three, four, a whole day. Whatever you say, *sahib*.' Their answer surprised me.

'But didn't the man explain that I am planning to go to Gangasagar?'

'Well, this is Gangasagar.'

'No, the Gangasagar where Ganga merges into the sea.' The two boatmen were a bit intrigued by my words and then, looking at each other in mutual complicity, they exclaimed in chorus:

'*Hare Gange, hare Gange…*'

'But why? Didn't the man tell you?' I was a shade intrigued by their answers.

'But, *sahib*, the Gangasagar you are talking about is beyond Calcutta.'

'Yes, that's why I said it was a long journey.'

'In that case, *sahib*, you should go to the railway station. Take the train to Saharanpur or Dehra Dun. From there, it's direct to Calcutta. In Calcutta, you might find someone to row you down to Gangasagar.'

'But didn't that fellow explain to you?' I clarified, 'I would like to do a boat-journey from Hardwar to Gangasagar.' The boatmen burst out laughing.

The more I tried to explain my project to them, the more I tickled their sense of humour. As I stood perplexed and discouraged by their attitude, the boatmen seemed to take me for someone who had lost his mind.

'I have an idea,' said one, sardonically, 'yes, a wonderful idea. *Do sulphe le lee jiye aur ganga ki ganga aap sagar pahunch jayenge*, two good joints of marijuana, and you'll go sailing right down to the sea!' Had they taken me for a drug-addict?

'But I'm serious, *bhaiya*,' I pleaded.

'So are we. Two joints and you'll be at Gangasagar.'

'Stop it!' I said, trying to put authority in my voice, 'you seem like novices at your job. I know of a couple who went down Ganga on a boat.'

'Well, they must have taken four joints, two for the man, two for the woman! There are many such foreigners in the *ashrams* of Rishikesh. Some go down Ganga, others up to the moon!'

I was getting impatient with the boatmen and about to leave when an old boatman walked out of a nearby hut and joined in our conversation. Rebuking the young boys for misbehaving with a stranger, he said to me:

'*Sahib*, we thought you probably wanted to rent a boat for some film shooting. There've been such cases in the past. But the boat-journey to Gangasagar is impossible. We've never heard of such a thing before.'

'Excuse me, *tauji*,' I addressed him with due respect, 'I've heard of a couple of people who have done this journey. I know it's not fairly common but...'

'How can it be? There's not enough water in Ganga. For eight months out of twelve, there's not enough water in Ganga even for a skim-boat. Yes, the only time it could be possible is after the monsoon, but then the currents of Ganga*ji* are too dangerous... Just the other day, one of our young boys got caught in a whirlpool and died. So you see...'

'Why is there no water in Ganga ?'

'Go ask the engineers. They have sucked it all out. We hear they are generating electricity but god knows where this electricity is because we haven't seen any in our huts so far. And let me tell you another thing. Don't ever think of going down Ganga*ji* over long distances. There's a lot of crime. Every other day we hear of murders and robberies. Fishermen get killed these days for a sum as small as ten rupees. So don't waste your time, young man, you can't do such a journey. There's neither water nor boatmen. But if you want a short fun trip, we are at your service.'

Disappointed, we drove back to the Inspection Bungalow in the hope that some competent engineer would be able to inform me of the navigable routes on Ganga. For three whole days I chased the engineers of the area. Mr. Srivastava, the Executive Engineer, was not in his office; his assistant was away to his daughter's hometown. Mr. Mittal, the Sub-Divisional Officer *sahib*, had a running nose and, therefore, could not receive any visitors while his colleague, Mr. Nigam, had left for a three-week long Tirupati pilgrimage. The only engineer in town was Mr. Aggarwal, but he was nowhere in sight. His peon said: 'He should be around somewhere in the building. His jacket is hanging on his chair and his briefcase is open.' And sure enough, for three long days, the jacket remained hanging and the briefcase yawned wide, but there was not a trace of the invisible man. After a few harrowing days with the Indian bureaucracy, I finally managed to get an appointment with a pompous and corrupt-looking senior engineer who talked to me as if he were interviewing me for a post in his office:

'You are not knowing Cotley?' he asked me, amazed at my lack of knowledge about the river.

'Cotley? Who's Cotley?'

'It is indeed surprising. You are not knowing Cotley!' he laughed mockingly.

'Which Cotley?'

'There is only one Cotley. Only.'

'Who is Mr. Cotley?'

'He is not Mr. Cotley. He is Colonel Cotley. He was a legend in the British colonial administration. And you are not knowing Colonel Cotley, and you're saying you're writing about Ganga!' I noticed that with each bump in his laughter, his stomach jumped up and down. Looking at his watch, he said to himself: 'Oh, the day is passing so fast!'

'You have another appointment, have you?'

'No, no. I am thinking it is lunch-time only.' From his looks, he could have safely skipped food for a whole month. 'Yes, Colonel Cotley, yes, was the man who first thought of constructing a canal on the Ganges only. If you have electricity today, it is because of him only. And if there is no water in the river, it's because we are sucking water from the river to generate power for our motherland. I hear you are wanting to go down Ganga in a...' Just then his peon knocked at the door and announced: '*Sahib*, Mr. Attari has come to meet you.' Distinctly unhappy at the idea of receiving another visitor before lunch, he commanded his peon:

'Tell him to come another day only. *Sahib* is leaving for an urgent tour, yes.' Looking at me, he picked up his line of thought and continued:

'To cut a long story small, you can't be rowing on Ganga with this much water only. If you have to be doing it–it's silly to be doing it in the first place–if the devil has asked you to do it, you must begin your journey at Sherpur only, where the canal will once again be throwing its waters into Gangaji... Yes, yes, write it down, at Sherpur. There is even a Hanuman temple at the...' The peon knocked at the door again and, before he could utter a word, the engineer screamed at him full throat: 'I've told you not to be disturbing me during an important meeting. Keep all the people waiting outside only. Bloody hell! All sorts of idiots and jokers are keeping walking in the whole day.' The peon, shrunk to half his size in fright, looked at him slavishly, and said: 'No, *sahib*, it's the *chote sahib* who wants to come in.' The *chote sahib*, in all likelihood, was the engineer's son. The peon had barely finished his sentence when a young dandy, dressed in bright red and white striped trousers, barged in through the open door and, with a clownish bow, greeted us:

'Good afternoon, Papa. Good afternoon, Sir!' Grabbing a chair, he looked at me, smiled, blinked, winked, cleared his throat, and said:

'I hear you're a foreign journalist.'

'Who told you that?'

'My mother told me that a foreign journalist was coming to meet Papa today. Is it true you're a journalist?'

'Well, I suppose I am.'

'Oh! How wonderful! I'm also a journalist. We have so much in common.' He winked again.

'Well, I'll leave you both with each other,' announced the engineer abruptly, 'I'll be back after lunch.'

'Sir, I am journalist with *Drona Vasundra*. It's a single-handed effort. I write it, I edit it, I publish it. I distribute it. One man show'

'Sounds great if you're not the only one who reads it.'

'Oh! We'll come to that later. I want to talk to you about certain discoveries that I've made. Give me a minute and I am sure that an intelligent person like you will appreciate what I've done. Now, you see, there are nine gates to the kingdom of knowledge: Two eyes, two nostrils, one mouth, two ears, one *lingadwar*–the little slit on your private part–and finally, one anus. The tenth gate is shut and that, everyone knows, is the…'

'But what are you getting at with these gates?' I exclaimed in exasperation. With his round, bulging eyes and trembling hands, the young boy, to say the least, looked mentally deranged.

'Don't be impatient. It takes some energy, effort and time to get to the kingdom of knowledge. Now the tenth gate is the navel, shut at the time of birth. Only a *yogi* can open it. But, in truth, there are fifteen gates to the kingdom of knowledge. Nine I have counted and, then, two testicles…'

'Whoever has a hole in his testicles?' I asked.

'Of course you have a hole in the testicles, but only a *yogi* can see it. So let's go back to the count. Two testicles, two breasts, open only in women, and one brain open only in men—and now, the fifteenth is the famous third eye which only Lord Shiv Shankar was gifted with…'

'But excuse me, *bhaiya*, I must…' I said, trying to get up from my chair.

'Sir, sir, sir… Be patient, big brother.' He opened the palm of his hand wide open and stuck it flat against my eyes. 'Just look, now. One, two, three, four… there are fifteen segments on the hand. But fifteen segments can be held together only by a sixteenth. And that is the circle. Now sixteen is the maximum number of qualities that a man can have. Lord Rama had mastered sixteen arts. These sixteen *kalas* are made of thirty-two parts. I'll show you which thirty-two. Just open your mouth…'

'What?' I gasped.

'Yes, yes, please. Please cooperate. Open your mouth wide. Don't worry, I won't hurt you.'

He stared at me in anticipation. When he realised that I was in no mood of obliging him, he opened his own mouth wide and said: 'Now you see, the thirty-two parts are the thirty-two teeth with as many openings. Ten I counted before. Another ten, the space between the nails and the skin, plus five others which I first counted. The third eye and another hole in the head from which *Gangaji* emerged. This makes forty-four. I have found two things in Biology. By the way, I am a first class first from Dehradun University. Man has $X+44$ chromosomes and woman, she has $X+44$. Sorry, $Y+44$. I have now found that by putting this together in equation, they cancel each other at sixteen. And that is exactly why when any two forms of life cross, they yield sixteen forms of life. Man and woman meet, there are sixteen forms of life. Mix two seeds, as our great agronomists have done, you have sixteen types of plants. To understand the notion of sixteen…'

'But what the hell do you want to do with this goddamned sixteen?'

'*Are!* Patience! You want proof. You see, sixteen indicates that all elements are the product of solar fission. The sun too has sixteen elements…'

I picked up my bag, thanked the mad son of a half-mad engineer, and ran for dear life. As I was leaving, he shouted after me: 'Pity, pity you didn't hear the conclusion, I would have proved to you that Christmas is a Hindu festival, and the Westminster Abbey is a Shiva temple!'

I told Mihir Singh that our next destination would be Sherpur, the only clue to the navigable course of Ganga that I had managed to pick up after a two-hour meeting. But on second thoughts, I thought of re-visiting my uncle in Rishikesh, who was after all also an engineer, and who might, with some luck, be able to find me a boat for my journey. We drove back to Rishikesh. My uncle had little to suggest, but he handed me a letter that had arrived the same morning. It was from Jaya.

amore mio,

your letter floated in, like nadja did a week ago, and i was yours like i have never been before. your letter was the magic lantern i was groping for. it was the sacred offering which my mother sent for the festival of deepawali and, sure enough, it arrived in a greasy envelope along with yours. what was 'us' about? why do i cry and laugh at the electric poetry of your words? where do i go to grope for images, impressions? i can but recreate, reinvent an optical screen on which to play in slow motion once, twice, ever so often, snatches from our autumnal past, a painful nostalgic backward glance held in suspension... i didn't expect you to write, not with such poignancy, and my defences crumbled, yes, collapsed like sand-castles on a desolate beach. you are the words, the time that rhythms my silence. wild petrified images come to my mind when I think of our last walk together in parc montsouris with autumn as our witness, shiva dancing in frenzied passion, his tandava in the crematorium grounds, dancing in the circle of stone where i wanted to photograph you. remember, dancing to destroy, dancing to create... hori bole...

did you know that montsouris was a vast necropolis?

my love, my young love, your letter is one of the most beautiful love poems i have ever read, it continues from where the 'serpent and the rope' ends and between illusion and reality, it is this brilliant shining space, where, once upon a time, a young prince, a marxist baul prince, met Cinderella who couldn't get into glass slippers but who made it into the salopette alright, but, then, does one ever live happily after?

nadja, my little feline acquisition, is adorable company. she has eyes like yours and i love to watch, as i did yours, her irises dilate into a full eclipse and then get back to being nothing but a feline slit. it is early morning and dawn is floating in on the wings of a pale insomnia.

i have searched for you à travers readings of nadja, l'amour fou and la revolution surréaliste. i watch the grass grow, i am on the beach on weekends, i write your name on the sands of time only to watch with growing sadness the waters creep up and obliterate...

to speak of the quotidian, for the first few nights i drank hot milk in solidarity with a parisian myth, my eyes were pouring rain, i was seeing you in bed next to me, calling your name, i didn't hear you snore though! it was so crazy, bewildering

'j'ai beau' crier que je t'adore

et ne suis rien que ton amant.'

i miss you and i enjoy this live, warm feeling of missing you...

nishant, take me the way i am. i cannot ask you to stay, i have no right to ask you to love me. love just 'is' and, one day, it will leave the way it tip-toed in. i can but offer you myself anointed with the sacred and the profane, i can offer you spangled dreams, that are and are not. i can offer you passionate sunsets, the colour of pomegranate blossoms, i can be your 'anarkali'. i can offer you space to come, to go, to stay, i can offer all that was destiny...

jaya

Boat-High

(pages from my diary, a night on Ganga)

THE BOAT IS ANCHORED. GANGA LAPS RHYTHMICALLY against its sides. A cool draft of wind makes the river erupt in passion. My notebook is fluttering wet. There's so much movement that it's impossible to write. Peer Singh has just managed to get a lantern going. Its kerosene smells in the yellow flame just as the flame dances on the faintly-lit shores of a somnambulist Ganga. I look at her waves, she smiles; I touch her waist, she takes my hand in hers. She's a coquette, this Ganga, whom history has made out to be a myth. Hidden in the foliage of a tree, a nightingale sings melancholically. As the wind rushes in, the bird appears to sit on my shoulder, and as the wind recedes, she becomes the sound of infinite horizons. Peer Singh and Ram, the boatmen, are sitting on the tail, laughing and chatting around a soothing *chilum* of grass.

It has been difficult to write all these days. So much has transpired, and often with such electric swiftness, that I've felt completely by-passed by the delirium of being. Since Jaya's letter a few days ago, Ganga has cast a strange magical spell on my mind. Her bounty has made me weep, laugh, repent, meditate, without allowing me a single respite of cognizance so that I could see myself from without. Ganga, like Jaya, has offered pleasure, bagfuls of it, with the gentle hint of wisdom that when you bathe dreams, it is best to shut doors on a rationalist curiosity. Between the poet and the poem, she said, there is a distance, a necessary gap. When you are a poem, live it. And when you are a poet, write it. The poem and the poet never belong to the same moment of time, just as love and lovers don't belong to the same moment of time. A poem exists in the poet for the poet cannot be the poem. To be a poem is to be Ganga, is to be Jaya. Only Jaya can offer humanity a 'rendezvous with destiny,' for rivers there are many, but Ganga there is one.

The journey began over five days ago. The beginning itself was not as easy as I had imagined. For three whole days before setting off, I shuttled frantically between Sherpur, a village on Ganga, and Bulandhshehr, the district headquarters, in a desperate bid to find two boatmen willing to accompany me down the river. For the larger part, the boatmen seemed utterly scared. Some feared murder and others, robbery. One was afraid of being home-sick, another pleaded ignorance of the tricky channels of Ganga. At last, a local *tehsildar* managed to virtually bribe two boatmen into rowing me some one hundred kilometres down the river. Despite the temptation of earning two thousand rupees for three days' work, Ram could still not be pulled out of his grudging reluctance. Falling prey to the bait of money, he agreed, but reminded the mighty *tehsildar*: 'Sahib, if you so order, I'm willing to accompany him. You are my master. If anything happens to my family, *sahib*, I'm sure your generosity will look after my wife and the children.' Saying this, he touched the *tehsildar's* feet in slavish respect. The officer responded with an arrogant laugh: 'Stop it, you silly fool! What could happen to anyone under the holy wings of Gangaji...'

The next morning, I woke up early, well before sunrise. The whole night I was tormented by delightful tall cliffs and vast stretches of blue waters running into the horizon, a vision that entered my dreams after my first holiday on the Peloponnesian coast. I had waited far too long for my little boat to be on Ganga, and the thought that this morning was to mark the beginning of my journey filled my eyes with tears. The *tehsildar's* driver drove me down to the banks of the river where Ram and Peer Singh were waiting for me, chewing the *neem* stick with relish. Seeing me, they jumped to their feet, and greeted me:

'*Jai Ramji ki, sahib, jai Ramji ki.*'

'*Jai Ramji ki.* All set for the journey?'

'Yes, *sahib*, all set. We've bought everything we need.'

'I hope it's enough. I don't want you to go hungry on the boat.'

'Should be enough, *sahib*. Ten kilos of wheat flour, three kilos of *arhar ki dal*, lentils, onions, garlic, spices, salt. Four litres of kerosene oil, a torch with four battery cells, one lantern. We thought you might need vegetables, so we've bought twelve kilos of potatoes.'

'What! Twelve kilos of potatoes!' I exclaimed.

'Yes, *sahib*, twelve. Ten for you, two for us.'

'O no! But our next stop is tomorrow.'

'Yes, *sahib*, but one feels hungrier on water. We've also bought ten bundles of *beedis* and two packets of cigarettes for you.' He handed me the cigarettes which offered me a choice between two brands, Red Lamp and Red and White.

'And the pots and pans?' I enquired.

'Yes, yes, we have enough to get by.'

'Water! Have you taken a pot of water?'

'Water?'

'Some drinking water.'

'But there's water all around us, *sahib*. It's an insult to the holy river to drink any other water than hers. This is the holiest water on earth: *payasvinin ghratinin mrityudhara*. Her water, *sahib*, is as pure as milk, as healthy as butter, and can deliver all souls to the heavens. Haven't you heard, *sahib,* that Gangaji can cure diseases that no modern doctor can? Malaria, cholera, plague, everything... We drink her water regularly. It keeps us healthy.' Out of respect for them, I gave ear to their beliefs, although I knew only too well that the *melas* on the banks of Ganga were the cause every other year of uncontrollable epidemics, above all, of cholera.

There was excitement in the air. As I spread a blanket on the wooden plank-seat dampened by morning dew, Ram carefully placed a framed picture of Lord Shiva on the inner side of the stern. Just then, a beautiful *sarus*-crane glided in with the wind and perched for a few seconds on Shiva's head. Pecking three times on the wooden frame, she then flew away, her black and white flapping giving a magnificent strobe effect to the morning sky. We were all set to leave when a woman, surrounded by five children, and with a *puja*-platter in her hand, came up to the bank. Thick tufts of incense smoke clouded her face and, behind it, I could hear some faint sobbing. Noticing their presence, Ram hopped out of the boat to meet his family, and before he could get close to them, the sobbing transformed into full-blown howling. Peer Singh, the proud and manly Rajput, found the whole sight a little too sentimental and womanly for his macho lineage. Sensing caste fraternity towards me, he whispered: 'Just look at him crying like a grandma! *Sahib,* Ram is from the caste of traders – a Bania. And a Bania remains a Bania all his life. Crying like a woman! *Hutt!*'

Ram was unperturbed.

With deep reverence, eyes shut and head bowed, he carried the fragrant smoke into each corner of the hull and then, with the grace of a dancer, he picked up the flame-yellow marigold petals and offered them, one by one, to the holy river. No sooner had the petals touched the surface than Ganga swept them under her swirling skirt and, with petals showing us the way, the boatmen plunged their oars to begin a journey where the mythical joins the real.

The boat slid swiftly, responding to the rhythm of the oars. Initially, Peer Singh took the oars while Ram was deputed the navigational task of looking out for possible shoals in the river. The draught in the river did not pose any problems, thanks to the feeder canal which had just poured her waters into Ganga, and with the spread of the river limited to a few hundred meters, the depth was quite rowable. Since the going was smooth, Ram was asked to quit navigation and join Peer Singh at the oars. As I sat back watching them row, I noticed that there was an amazing correspondence between the moods of the river and those of the boatmen: a smooth going made them hum and sing, while the slightest drop in water-level made their faces anxious and tense. 'A boatman is his river's slave, *sahib*,' said Peer.

The sun rose, making large luminous holes in the wintry mist. The birds came out in hundreds, twinkling like stars in the sky. As the cranes, gulls and sparrows sang to awaken the goddess from her nightly bed, the partridges and sparrows in the fields announced to the farmer the dawn of yet another day.

A few minutes of sun was enough to create an atmospheric lightness which made the wind rush in from the back. Feeling the wind in the oars, the boatmen looked at each other and exclaimed: '*Haisha, haisha,* pull hard, my friend. Let her fly like a bird,' and they began to sing a melancholic song from the film *Kabuliwala*.

Suddenly the boat bumped against something nasty and the boatmen cried out in alarm: '*Arre, are, hare Ram…*' It seemed that the boat had hit a stone reef, but Peer Singh was more worried about the damage than about what had caused the accident. He took off his pyjamas and jumped into the river. 'Thank God,' he said reassuringly, 'we're lucky. Just a scratch!' After a few minutes of anxiety, we resumed our journey. The water-level was considerably reduced and we now had to keep a constant watch for the rowable channel within Ganga. An immediate reordering of the rowing pattern was worked out. Leaving the oars to Ram, Peer Singh went and stood on the stern. With one hand arched to shade his eyes from the sun, he guided the boat on the unpredictable river. I tried to help Ram with the oars but my lack of synchronization appeared more of a nuisance than relief. They asked me to sit back and relax and, if I insisted, to peel the onions.

Very soon, the river became a source of great worry for the boatmen. The cruising speed had virtually dropped down to zero and, at times, was even negative, for frequently, the navigable channel within the river ran diametrically against the direction in which the river was flowing. There were times when the water-level dropped down to a few centimetres, and we had to drag the boat to a point where the level made rowing possible again. Following a curious serpentine path, making its way through patches of golden sand on which the first creepers were showing signs of birth, our boat crossed the bridge at Garhmukhteshwar and made slow headway towards a destination that was best left to the realm of the unknown.

The shoals were a rare treat to the eye. Small tanned mounds floated like shapely breasts on the pale green surface of the water. To Ganga herself, the shoals were a mere reminder that she was probably the heaviest of all the rivers on earth. A nineteenth century Victorian engineer, Sir Charles Lyell, once estimated that Ganga deposited some 350,000,000 tons of silt, nearly the weight of sixty replicas of the great pyramid at Ghazipur, half way down the length of the river. If the sand deposits were that heavy way down the river, in ranges closer to her source,

Ganga deposited even larger quantities of silt and, in so doing, rendered the river virtually impossible for normal transportation. Even during the pioneering expeditions of the early nineteenth century, Prinsep, while preparing reports for the British steam companies based in Calcutta, considered Garhmukhteshwar to be the last reachable station upstream. So sticky and dangerous was the hazard posed by the shoals that the British companies employed special squads of workers, posted all along the upper regions, to sound bell-alarms for the upstream traffic of the East India Company.

The shoals had ruled out any possibility of cooking. Seeing the boatmen exhausted, I offered them bread and *Amul* cheese cubes. Ram observed me biting into my cheese and then, holding his cube close to the nose, enquired:

'What's this, *sahib?* Looks like soap.' Out of politeness, he popped the little block of cheese into his mouth. Seeing me absorbed in my lunch, he stealthily turned his back to me and rinsed his mouth out with some water.

Once past Parora and the bathing pilgrims at the Harihar Baba temple, the going became smooth. Peer Singh and Ram took turns at the oars. Helped by the late afternoon breeze from the west, the boat seemed to be cruising at a speed that left little to desire. Our rough target for the day had been Tikadevi temple and its famous *baba* who, I was told, had been meditating on the holy banks for many years. If Ganga's mood swings did not betray us any further, the hope of reaching our destination was indeed not remote. We pressed on further.

The sun had become less hot and light was beginning to fade. The manly Rajput and the gentle Bania, were both starting to show signs of fatigue. Nobody really knew the exact distance we had to cover. Anxious to reach a safe halt by nightfall, we pulled the boat towards a local fisherman and asked him:

'*Bhaiya*, how far is it to the Tikadevi temple?'

'Not too far. There's a straight bus from Garh to the temple.'

'No, no, along Gangaji. How far is it?'

'But there's no fish there.'

'We couldn't be going fishing at night, could we?' said Peer, impatiently. 'How far is it by the river?'

'Only Gangaji can tell you,' he answered. 'Never been there.'

'What's the next village…?'

'Bhonra, Sherpur…'

'But these are upstream villages!' Peer Singh cut him short rudely.

'Ah! You're going downstream, are you? Hang on, let me think.' For five long minutes, he counted and re-counted villages on the finger-tips of his mind, and then, with the embarrassed look of a back-bencher in the face of a difficult question, he admitted apologetically: 'I don't know. I don't belong here. This is my father-in-law's village. You seem to be going far. You'd better hurry because the birds are about to return home.'

Birds are the only clock that the lonely traveller on Ganga has ever known. It is their infallible sense of intuitive time that keeps Ganga and her pilgrim moving along the paths of timelessness. Birds awaken the sun, as they awaken you, and then, when the sun dips, it is they who ask the boatman to gather his nets. Without birds, Ganga is unthinkable.

Within minutes, the sun transformed the river into a tunnel of orange fire. Thousands and thousands of birds, these alarm-clocks of another world, invaded the sky. A million elliptical curves transformed the sky into a schoolboy's sketch-book and, for a few minutes, the sky looked like an enchanting lesson on the geometry of disorder. Cranes, storks, gulls and sparrows dipped low over the river-goddess and, kissing her farewell, they landed their matchstick legs on the soft shoals. As twilight descended in her azure costume, cranes strolled like mannequins on the shoals. The *chakva* and the *chakvi*, the Romeo and Juliet of the amorous bird-world, sang in the distance the song of their immortal love. Blue, green, red, white, the birds merged colour, gesture and sound, to present just one fragment of that bewitching opera which the cosmos announced on the day the earth quit her ancestral abode in the solar ball. The last romantic on this earth—a sea-gull gliding before a naked blue sky...

If the silence of the birds signalled nightfall, we too had covered our distance in good time. We had crossed the pontoon bridge at Anupshehr and, beyond the faint glow of neons, the Tikadevi temple stood smiling over the right bank. A gas lamp, placed in the temple grounds, lit the front facade of the temple. Apart from that, there was little sign of life. For the tired boatmen, it sufficed that we had reached our destination. Dropping the oars in the boat with a sign of relief, Ram exclaimed: 'Now let Ganga carry us to the temple! I've done this job since childhood but never have been so tired as today!' The infatigable and the ever-alert Peer Singh jeered: 'Come on, you Bania, stop complaining like a woman! Think of what you have to do. Think of cooking some food for *sahib*.' Through minute details and passing remarks, Peer Singh revealed the whole tale of caste mentalities in rural India.

'*Sahib*, we'll take the boat across to the bank, cook and eat there. Then we can anchor midstream to sleep,' Ram suggested.

'Sleep on the boat?' I asked, 'It's too small. We'll sleep out there on the bank.'

'No, no, *sahib*. The times are bad,' cautioned Ram, 'there are incidents of robbery and crime everyday. No, I wouldn't advise that.' I thought Ram was overreacting, but Peer Singh agreed with him: 'He's right, *sahib*, we shouldn't sleep on the bank. There've been cases where a boatman was robbed of five rupees.

There are criminals among the boatmen caste itself. We should anchor midstream.'

'How will that help? The man can reach us midstream too!'

'To catch someone on water is always tougher, *sahib*. It gives us time to prepare.' The whole thing was beginning to sound a bit sinister.

'But what if the attackers are armed...' I laughed to dilute the tension.

'It's not that simple, *sahib*. We're prepared too. We've made our own arrangements...' Peer Singh moved to the stern and pulled out three balls from a cloth-bag, hidden behind Lord Shiva's idol.

'What is this?'

'*Laddus, sahib!*' exclaimed Peer Singh, playfully.

'What is it?'

'Country bombs! Good enough to blast a boat! We have to protect ourselves, *sahib*. Otherwise life would be impossible in this profession.' He put the bombs carefully back into the cloth-bag and muttered to himself: 'Hope they haven't got wet, my little *laddus*...'

I had a wash in the cold river water while Ram and Peer Singh, undressed to their *caleçons*, went into Ganga to dissolve the day-long fatigue. By the time they returned, with marigold petals clinging to their bodies, it was dark. Peer Singh quickly lit a small fire and Ram got busy chopping onions, garlic, green chillies and potatoes. 'You don't mind chillies in the food I hope,' inquired Ram.

'On the contrary, I love them.' Barely had I finished expressing my love for spices and chillies when Ram threw a fistful of green chillies into the frying pan. Peer Singh filled himself a *chilum* while I took out my sleeping bag and stretched out on the bank.

I looked up towards the clifftop temple which, until not

very long ago, had looked deserted. Now a human shadow had appeared on the temple wall. The shadow resembled a graffiti or an advertisement for hair oil. As I was looking at the wall, the shadow moved. It seemed to recline against a pillar, now bending its body over, so as to hold its feet in its hands. Then, the shadow moved again, tossing its head backwards. I noticed long hair. A long-haired *sadhu*? Or a woman? It was like watching a slide-show, where images changed quickly. The shadow moved again. It got up and walked gently out of the screen. A little later, the screen itself disappeared, for the lamp had either been removed or covered with a cloth. A heavy translucence hung over the contours of the temple.

I decided to climb the cliff to investigate. Just then, the shadow chose to reveal itself. A woman, with a lamp in one hand, walked up to the edge of the cliff. Upright, free, confident, like Athena, she looked deep into the infinity of Ganga. Strange, a goddess on the banks of the holy Ganga? A divine encounter on the tracks of a mysterious river...

She put the lamp on a rock and away from the glare of light, she sat down, a picture of ultimate mystery. Legs half-folded, chin on her knees, contemplating the horizon.

'Who is she?' I asked Peer Singh.

'*Malum nahin*,' whispered Peer, 'let's mind our own business.'

'Strange, but who could she be?' I persisted.

'Let's drop the subject *sahib*. Tell me, would you like some salad with the meal?' Peer Singh was obviously trying to divert my attention from the woman.

'Peer, I'd like to go up and talk to her.'

'Don't,' snapped Peer Singh. 'Don't be crazy, *sahib*. You can't trust anyone these days. It might just be a dirty trick being played on us. Let's eat and find a safe place to sleep. Times are really bad *sahib*, and this whole area is infested with dacoits and bandits.'

'Come off it, Peer Singh. This woman looks quite harmless. She might even have lost someone in her family.'

'May well be. But who knows what's hidden behind? Tell me, would you fancy some salad with your dinner?'

Just then we heard the girl hum the first line of a famous Urdu *ghazal*. Ram and Peer Singh looked at each other, suspecting a plot. She hummed beautifully.

'I want to go and meet her.' I told the boatmen.

'No, *sahib*. Please don't.' Both of them said emphatically.

'There's no point asking for trouble. God alone knows who she is. A mad woman? Someone's wife? Could be anyone. And frankly *sahib*, there have been far too many murders in the area for us to take such instances lightly. We beg of you. Don't.' Peer Singh had suddenly become so protective and cautious in his manner that there was indeed very little of the proud and manly Rajput left in his personality.

I picked up my pack of cigarettes and walked up to the top of the cliff. She was dressed in a tight *salwar-kameez*. A light, white cloth covering her bust, fluttered nervously in the breeze. She was slim and shapely, and her long dark hair let loose to the madness of the wind covered her left shoulder. Nervous, having pushed myself into a situation which I could neither enter nor get out of, I approached her hesitantly from the side. With a natural grace, she turned towards me. She had a wheatish complexion, dark almond eyes, high cheek bones. There was a youthful radiance on her face. Before I could say anything, she turned her face back towards the river. I heard the boatmen whispering something to each other.

'*Adabarzhai*,' she greeted me in flawless Urdu, still staring into the horizon.

'*Adab*,' I greeted her back. I sat down at some distance from her.

'You like distances, don't you.' Her remark disarmed me completely. '*Aap ki tareef?*' she asked.

'Nishant. I am a traveller. Going down Ganga on a boat.'

'Ganga?'

'Well, Ganga*ji.*'

'Pilgrim?'

'If you like.'

'A journey down Ganga? This has to be a pilgrimage.'

'Yes,' I uttered clumsily. 'I'm planning to write a book. *Aur aap ki tareef?* And you? What's your...'

'Zehra.' One word answer. Rose. So she was Muslim.

'Do you live here?' I tried to lighten the weight of silence.

'Oh no! I came here for the *mela*. There was a *mela* here two days ago. I stayed on.'

'So, you've come to wash your sins, too?' I asked.

'That could be one way of putting it.' She turned her face away and, again, looked deep into the night. Breaking the silence, she mumbled: 'Yes, to wash a few sins and to commit a few more.' She burst out laughing. Her laughter, her crisp and poetic answers, left me speechless. Who was she? Illusion? Reality? Magician? *Sanyasini?* Ganga?

'Where do you live then?' I persisted.

'Meerut. Do you know Meerut?'

'Yes, a bit. What do your parents do?'

'Nothing. But I work.'

'Not many women work in our country.'

'But for some, it is necessity.'

'So what do you do?'

'Love.' She looked into my eyes and laughed again. I heard the boatmen whisper again.

'You seem to be poet.' She smelt of poetry through each pore.

'O no! Poets write, I can't even write. I've never been to school.'

'But there are poets who never went to school!'

'They are dreamers, not poets.'

'What do you do? Because love is the profession of a poet.'

'*Shair sher se muhabbat karte hein, ham shair se muhabbat karte hain. Shair khwab se muhabbat karte hein, ham unke jism se muhabbat karte hein. Farq hai dono baton mein.* Poets love poems but I love the poet. A poet loves his dreams, but I love the poet's body. There's a slight difference between the two professions. Yes, I trade in song and flesh.' She chortled, as if to admire her own prose, and turning around, looked at me straight in the eye with a fire which melted my last defence. She spoke in metaphors. Her glance had the poetic precision of geometry. Her silences made me a prisoner of her words. In her speech, her eyes, her wrists, the twirl of her lips, Zehra carried the stamp of matchless poetry. If the world chose to call her an immoral prostitute, may all women be prostitutes; if the world chose to call her a moral untouchable, may she be the goddess of the holy touch, for Zehra was nothing but that priceless gift that Ganga offers to the seeker of her destiny. I abandoned myself completely into the hands of the unknown. I looked into the night, and said, hurl defiance to the stars...

'You like silence, don't you?' she remarked teasingly.

In truth, I chose silence because I wished Zehra to speak ceaselessly in her enchanting phonemes. What a marvellous language Urdu is, so intensely musical that music becomes a part of the language itself. Urdu dissolves music. Like a symphony, its sounds emerge like infinite ripples, each connected to the other, creating a harmony where even disorder has an order. If Urdu was music, then Zehra was its youngest and most dangerous exponent. 'Come closer, why are you sitting that far.' She smiled and then, stretching her neck like a swan, looked into the starlit night. 'What a beautiful night! Each star has turned out for the celestial procession! If you like, we could go for a walk...'

Ram and Peer Singh were huddled together in one long, black blanket. I went down to tell them that I would not be back until later. The boatmen were shocked to hear that I had accepted her invitation for a stroll. Peer Singh, playing on our common caste fraternity, was so embarrassed that he pleaded with me: '*Sahib*, such company does not reflect well on your respectable ancestry. And God forbid *sahib*, if something untoward were to take place, the *tehsildar* would put us behind bars. Don't go *sahib*.' I picked up another pack of cigarettes and left. As I climbed back towards Zehra, the loyal boatmen could be heard imploring: '*Sahib, sahib*, listen, *sahib*...'

She took the lamp and put it back on the temple doorstep where it probably belonged. Whispering '*Chalo, come*,' she led the way. I followed. It must have been fairly late at night. The moon shone silver bright, lighting the way for an ethereal stroll. The village to our right was fast asleep. The dogs, the cattle, the birds—their collective silence made them accomplices in an act for which there would not even be the King's witness. The only sound was the intermittent plopping of fish which receded as we moved away from the river. We went past the village and then crossed a mango-orchard. 'Avoid the main tracks and for the rest, just follow me,' she whispered in my ear. Zehra walked confidently, like a professional guide to the wilds. She pulled her white *dupatta* over her head. The cover of veil implies coyness, shyness, distance from the other. A cultural symbol, the *dupatta* is meant to lend dignity and respectability to a woman.

I noticed that the wild bushes through which we were walking were wet with dew. My jeans were soaked wet and I could feel the cold seep into my legs. Zehra seemed unconcerned. We must have walked fairly long, jumping over numerous fences and hurdles. After taking a rather circuitous track which seemed to lead us away from Ganga, I was surprised to find ourselves end up on top of a cliff overlooking the river. Rivers, I noticed, behaved differently under the touch of moonlight. There was an unusual turbulence in the waters. We sat down.

'*Ise bhooton ki ghat kehte hein*, this is where the ghosts bathe,' said Zehra, laughing. There was a peculiar metallic depth and seduction to her laughter. As I lay watching Ganga, she turned towards me and said: '*Bhoot, bhoot*, ghost.' She rounded her mouth and her eyes, and with her hands arched around her face, she started giggling:

'Ghosts, are you afraid of ghosts?'

'But fear is a ghost.' I remarked.

'What?'

'The moon is a ghost.'

'The star is a ghost.'

'The sky is a ghost.'

'The mango is a ghost.'

'The priest is a ghost.'

'The temple is a ghost.'

'Gangamaya is a ghost.'

'*Ma* is a ghost.'

'Sham is a ghost.'

'Rajiv is a ghost.'

'Indira Gandhi is a ghost.'

'*Nauka* is a ghost.'

'*Dhokha* is a ghost.'

'Your pimp is a ghost.'

'Your boatman is a ghost.'

'Your voice is a ghost.'

'Your eyes are a ghost.'

'Love is a ghost.'
'The night is a ghost.'
'Memory is a ghost.'
'Man is a ghost.'
'Jaya is your ghost.'
'Who?'
'Jaya is Zehra's ghost.'
'What?'
'Your eyes are a ghost.'
'Your mouth is a ghost.'
'Beckett is a ghost.'
'Who?'
'Godot is a ghost.'
'Who?'
'Your lips are a ghost.'
'Your eyes are a ghost.'
'Your lips are a ghost.'

She touched my lips, and Ganga smiled. She turned, ran, and in a flash, jumped into the river. I followed. The water was cold, freezing cold. Zehra was warm, warm like a silken flame. There comes a point in life when the hot and the cold, the sane and the insane, like all opposites, cease to be contradictory and the pagan egg-shell is born...

Love for her was homage. It was *puja*, dissolution of the self. It was search. Abandoning herself completely like a *sanyasini*, she cried, laughed, scratched and teased. Starved for a morsel of loving flesh, she bit me sky-blue. '*Allah mian, tumne yeh muhabbat kyon banayi, kyon banayi, kyon banayi,* Oh! Allah! Why did you create love on earth, why, why!' Deep as I was inside her being, she trembled and shook like a leaf. 'You have sought me too far. It is here, the *nirvana*, it is here, the *moksha*, it is here, the *maya*.' She produced a shattering magical sound. It came from deep within, from the echo-chambers of the abdomen and as her sound rose towards the sky, it evoked a lyre-bird fleeing a morning hunter. It was the sound of being, of infinity, of the self. It was Om. '*Maine barson se duniyan ko muhabbat dee hai, aaj pahli martaba kisi ajnabi ne mera udhar chukaya hai.* For years I have given love to men, for once, today, a stranger has paid back their debt.' She dug her nails deep into my waist and said in a voice that put the gods on trial: 'Allah! *Yeh meri nanhi si muhabbat ko na cheen,* Allah, don't snatch this young love from me.'

'You've been quiet for so long.' I noticed that I had fallen asleep. The glow of dawn slowly coloured the sky. Zehra wanted me to reveal myself. There was little to reveal. Zehra for me was an incredible *fareb*–mystery and truth in their moment of unity. Two years earlier, the 26th of October 1983, on the windswept cliffs of the English Channel, at Etretat, I had met the same woman the same way at the same hour. She was called Jaya. Zehra, the first name of tragedy is union...

'Quiet again. Come, say something,' said Zehra.

'I was just thinking.'

'What?'

'I didn't know that I had dozed off.'

'Tell me, what are you thinking of?' She nudged me with her elbow.

'A dream. I dreamt something. I dreamt about you. Strange dream.'

'What?'

'*You were in a forest. Perhaps a forest close to Ganga. Hair dishevelled, clothes torn, a baby bleeding in your arms, you were running, running frantically, as if trying to escape. Then, a king...*'

'Did you say a king?'

'*Yes, a king... The king was trying to capture you. His horsemen, hundreds of them, were chasing you. This went on for a while. I remember your face. A face after a murder. The king managed to catch up with you. By now, you had reached the banks of a river. He knelt before you and cried: "You've destroyed six of my children. One by one, you've thrown them into the river. Zehra, Zehra, I beg of you not to be so cruel and leave our last child to live and take my throne. I beg of you." The king pleaded and begged but you just stared at him with cruel red eyes and said: "You've broken your promise. The price of this breach is that this child shall also go the way of the others." You took the child and hurled him high into Ganga with a scream.* Huh! What a horrible dream!'

'Strange,' she said with a smirk, as if she had known the king, 'that was King Shantanu.'

'Which Shantanu?'

'Do you know the *Mahabharata*?'

'Yes'

'Do you know it well?'

'Well, who doesn't? But what exactly are you implying?'

'The *Mahabharata* begins with your dream. The famous encounter between Ganga and King Shantanu.'

'So Zehra in my dream was actually Ganga?'

'And King Shantanu was you!' Zehra laughed, giving me her hand.

In the course of a night, a pact had been signed between two desires, each as blind as the other. Zehra invited me to visit her hometown, Meerut. Since there was no direct bus from the Tikadevi to Meerut, we decided to boat it to the Kanpur-Agra bridge downstream and then work out the route to her city known for its famous 'Sepoy Mutiny' of 1857.

I returned to the boat to see that the friendly ambience of the day before had suddenly turned hostile. A funereal silence engulfed us. Ram and Peer Singh both wore a look of shock and insult. They felt let down. I had debased their moral honour. I must have been on the boat for over five minutes, but neither of them wished me the habitual greeting of friendship. There was a heavy silence as if someone had died. Yes, something had died: it was their faith in my respectability.

Within minutes, the ignominious world of social barriers had risen to the surface of a Ganga whose waters had flowed singing hymns to human equality. To the boatmen, Zehra was a 'shady woman'. Not only was she a prostitute in their mind, she was also the mistress of their moneyed master who had to be accorded the same respect that employers' women command in life. Things became worse, when Zehra addressed me in her polished Urdu and they discovered she was also a Muslim. Whore, moral untouchable, Muslim, the disaster for the boatmen was complete.

'There's some tea, *sahib*. Will you have some tea?' Ram made the offer while Peer Singh chose to look occupied.

'And you?' I asked, 'Have you had tea?'

'Yes, we have.'

'Well, then could we have two glasses of tea please?'

'There's just one glass for you, *sahib*,' Peer Singh half-snapped, looking at Zehra through the corner of his eye.

'In that case, we'll share the glass,' I asserted firmly. Peer dropped his glance.

Oppressed by the power of a master, the boatmen had little option but to take the oars towards a destination where Ganga led us next. The tensions between a prostitute-poetess and two Hindu conservatives had marred the charm of another morning on Ganga. I noticed the birds chirp and play on the shore, the sun spread a mat of light on the gentle waves, the vast expanse of Ganga light up like a mirror, but the tensions had stolen from me my quiet. We must have been on the boat for over half-an-hour when the boat crossed the *ghat* on which Zehra and I had spent the night. As we rowed past, Zehra drew towards me: 'Look! Bhooton ki ghat! Are you still afraid of the ghosts?' She got up, picked up a flower from the platter before Shiva's idol, and gently threw it towards the *ghat*. I was pensive, disturbed. Zehra sensed my introspection and, nudging me with her elbow, whispered:

'What's come over you? Why get angry with your men? I deal with such men every day. These are the ones who at night plead and kneel before my body. They curse their wives, they open their hearts out to me and, the morning after, refuse to look me in the eye. So you see, my love, Zehra needs but one face. It's they who need two. Hey! Look, look, a white rabbit in the bush!'

We reached the bridge in good time. The noon sun shone on us. I asked Peer Singh to pull the boat by the bank. 'I'm going to Meerut for two days, Peer, I'll be back the day after tomorrow. We shall continue the journey to Narora thereafter.'

Peer Singh looked stunned.

'I have some work in Meerut,' I repeated, 'I'll be back the day after.'

'You mean you're getting off here at the bridge!'

'Yes, but I'll be back.'

'This wasn't in the deal, *sahib*. We were asked to drop you at Narora. We didn't settle for any extra night-halts with the *tehsildar*. I'm sorry, *sahib*, this won't do.' For the first time, Peer Singh was outright curt.

'Look, *bhaiya*, I'm not here on some fun boat-ride. I am on work. If you like, we can re-negotiate the rates. What will you charge for the night-halt?'

'No, *sahib*. It's very kind of you to suggest this but we would like you to settle our account. That leaves us both free. You can go for your fun and we can return to our families.'

'I'm sorry I can't pay you right now.' I decided to take the tough line. And then in a last bid to reconcile, I asked:

'Tell me, are you angry with me?'

'No, *sahib*, but...'

'But what?'

'No, *sahib*, you won't understand but...'

'Here! Two hundred rupees for the halt and there's enough to eat on the boat.' Peer Singh accepted the money grudgingly while Ram looked rather pleased with the new arrangement. Rubbing a hundred rupee note gently between his thumb and the index finger, Ram said obediently. 'Fine, *sahib*. See you day after tomorrow. We'll be anchored right here.'

The bus was crowded, particularly because of the Hindu wedding season; and the next general elections were round the corner. Zehra and I managed to push our way through the front door. There was little room to stand, let alone sit. We stood in the aisle while the conductor kept asking us to move further down. Zehra squeezed herself through, attracting a thousand curious gazes. A youngish college student got up and pointing towards Zehra, said to me: 'You can ask her to sit down,' Quick and frothy as ever, Zehra accepted the offer and took the seat, covering her head with her *dupatta*. The trick of the veil on her head worked rather well and a conservative-looking man next to her, with a thick red mark on his forehead, thinking that we were a newly married couple, offered me his seat. I hesitated but his insistent politeness forced me to take the seat. Zehra smiled at him and the man blessed her: 'May you live long, may you live long, my daughter.' Had he known what Zehra did in real life, he would have rushed for a holy dip in Ganga!

The people around us were discussing the upcoming general elections. Their accents, their white *dhotis*, their headgear, everything about them betrayed that they were Jats and we didn't have to listen to them too carefully to realise that they were engaged in a popular critique of ruling the Congress party. An elderly Jat, clutching a solid stick in his hand, turned around and said to the passenger behind him: 'Take it from me, this young lad, Rajiv, has already won the elections! The elections are a mere formality.'

'What do you expect!' replied the other, exasperated. 'Our voter is a fool! If my mother were assassinated, he'd put me on the throne too.'

Clearing his throat, a young man snarled: 'This Prime Minister's seat has become the private property of the Nehru family. Nehru, then Indira, now Rajiv, and who knows, if he dies, his ten-year-old might rule this country of womanly souls!' The passengers burst out laughing.

'You laugh and giggle like women, you fools,' rebuked an old great-grandfatherly man, wheezing and coughing. 'You should be ashamed. There's no unity among you. You're divided! Good for nothing. Else how could the cowardly Brahmins rule over a country of warriors?' Another passenger joined in, adding his bit to the rustic macho discussion:

'I have no idea if this boy Rajiv will win or lose, but have you heard him speak on the radio? His mother sounded more manly!' The whole bus went into splits of laughter.

I was busy enjoying the gossip, when Zehra pinched me on my forearm and whispered:

'Listen.'

'What?'

'Oof! Bend down a bit, I'm not going to announce it to the whole bus, am I?' I lowered my face. Zehra's face looked wicked and mischievous. She pointed towards someone with her eyebrows:

'You see that man?'

'The guy next to the driver?'

'No, the man with a tie.'

'What about him?'

'He is the *bara sahib* in Meerut.' *Bara sahib* could be any high officer in the state administration.

'What kind of *bara sahib?*'

'I'm not sure about that,' said Zehra, giggling, "but he has a big house, lots of servants, and two telephones.'

'What about him?'

'I know him.' Zehra said aloud.

'Softly, softly. They can hear us.'

'And you know what? One night he called me over for five hundred rupees. A real horny old man. He uses aphrodisiacs!'

'Go and say hello to him.' I said teasingly.

'Don't be silly! You think he'd recognize me here?... But he's such a lovely old fool. One day, he asked me to come and see him. His family was away, so he thought of having some fun. When things were over, he asked me to sing. I sang him a Mirza Ghalib *ghazal*. Teasing him, I said now it's your turn to sing. And guess what?'

'He was too shy to sing.'

'No. He said he could sing but he would have to gargle first. He went and gargled. Then, what did he sing?'

'What?'

'Guess?'

'A film song?'

'No. Another guess.'

'A folk song.'

'No. Another guess.'

'A prayer.'

'Give up! He sang the national anthem! In all seriousness as if he were singing for the Republic Day parade!' Zehra looked at the man piteously and said: 'Poor chap! Such a pathetic old man.'

'Why do you say that?'

'Oh, if only you knew! He wants to make love forever but he can't. At times he says he has fever. At others, he says he has high blood-pressure!' Zehra burst out laughing, unable to control her girlish excitement. I looked around. The whole bus was staring at us. Luckily, just then, the driver drove into the Meerut bus terminal and we threw our bags into the first rickshaw that came our way.

It was late evening. The shops in the Meerut *bazaar* were about to shut. Smell of spices and herbs filled the congested and narrow alleys of the city. In one shop a gunny-bag of red chillies had split open. Everyone, sellers, buyers, passers-by, were coughing. After the quiet of Gangetic twilights, the humdrum of the Meerut bazaar hit hard on the nerves. Seeing me a bit disturbed by the crowded streets, Zehra asked the rickshaw-puller to take a quieter route, past the Sarafa Bazaar and Koocha Neel, until we reached the clock-tower. Zehra asked the man to stop and, slipping a two rupee note in his hand, said to me: '*Chalo,* come, quick.' I followed her. Just then, a Nepalese girl standing beside a shop, smiled at me. I knew I had entered Zehra's world of work.

I followed Zehra through a gate which resembled more a large hole in the wall. 'Come on up, hurry,' said Zehra, taking a staircase, or what was meant to be a staircase. It was just a heap of stones of all shapes and sizes, dumped on top of each other and leading somewhere further up into the darkness. I didn't know where to head. It was black as hell. 'Come, come.' 'Where are you? I can't see a thing.' 'Don't worry about that. Just come.' 'Hey, Zehra, give me your hand.' 'Not here, silly! Just feel the steps and climb.' I managed a few steps, stumbling and bumping against empty cans that produced a metallic clatter. As

I took the second flight of steps, someone with a sharp-as-knife voice spoke into my ear: 'Who are you?' Zehra explained that I was a friend, and I guessed that the faceless interlocutor of my identity was a watch-dog pimp.

Zehra was a picture of confidence. She moved freely. Her voice had command. She asked me if I would care for a cup of tea, and promptly ordered one of the girls to bring two cups. To liven up the atmosphere, she switched on the transistor and we were enveloped in blaring Hindi film music.

'Zehra, do you run this place?'

'O no! Come, I'll introduce you to aunty. She is the owner.'

We walked down another narrow, dingy corridor. Aunty was an enormous lady who god could have deprived of anything in life except flesh. Pounds and pounds of flesh, like tumorous lumps, hung from her cheeks, neck, breasts, waist, arms and had she not been exceptionally tall, she would have run the danger of being the most perfect sphere of flesh that I had ever seen in my life.

Aunty greeted me with a wide-mouthed smile: 'Welcome, welcome.' As she spoke, a viscous red blob of chewed betel leaf slipped from the edge of her mouth and dropped straight onto the floor. In a move utterly natural, she stamped out the liquid with her toe, leaving behind a crimson stain on the floor which resembled the colour of her own mouth.

Housed in a dilapidated mansion dating back to the turn of the nineteenth century, the brothel was a labyrinth, connecting one part of the building to another through a series of ingenious tricks of geometry. Just as in some Parisian architecture, a small gate leads to hidden *escaliers,* which, in turn, hide behind them other staircases and courtyards, the little black hole of the Meerut *kotha,* too, was only an entry-point to a more spacious graveyard of flesh-trade. At times the walls had been pulled down to create space, and through fabric partitions, a string of cubicles had been erected for the lovers of a fugitive night. Wet rags, humid scum, suffocating dust, smell of oil, cheap make-up and the sound of nervous giggling and laughter summed up the destiny of this *kotha*. A peculiar stench of decadence and death floated above the barbaric ejaculations of the human condition.

Zehra offered to show me around. I followed her with gingerly footsteps, as if walking through a morgue. The brothel was living its peak hour. Each cubicle produced loud, audible comments and if the prostitutes sounded vulgar and foul in their language, the men were worse. 'For ten rupees, you bitch, you could at least take off your shirt!' The man was apparently excited. The woman snapped back at him: 'If you get violent, I'll chop your prick and pack it up for your wife'. We turned into another corridor where a woman was pulling herself out of the grasp of a hefty middle-aged man: 'Enough, enough, leave some *masala* for your wife before she runs away with your neighbour.' Barely had she finished her phrase when the client in the next cabin let out the ultimate cry of a satiated man: 'Uh! Uh! Uh! Your mouth, your mouth! Don't remove that. Uh! Your mouth!'

Yes, it's true that there is a sense of tragicomic humour about such places. The humour stems from a peculiar 'freedom' shared by both the object and the subject. The man feels 'free' because he is free of any emotional attachment. His lack of inhibition and primitive abandon is rooted in the fact that he has paid for the object of his sexual pleasure. More than love, which demands reciprocity, sex bought is completely free. Money buys you a perverse freedom, the feeling that the commodity, or the woman, is inalienably yours. If the man in a brothel feels free because he has bought her services, the prostitute, the nightly nightingale, feels free because she has been dead since the very day she landed in this work-place. The prostitute's freedom is a negation of her self, it stems from a complete annihilation of her being. Man has forced her to gamble, to gamble freely, with joy and laughter. The tragedy about a brothel is the sordid truth that for both, the woman and the man, it is a space of absolute illusion, and it is in this illusion that they find their ghostly freedom. 'Smiles are there where wrinkles have been.' Was that Mark Twain?

Suddenly we heard the sound of an altercation. Somebody was screaming at the top of his voice: 'Thieves, thieves, a bunch of thieves. You ugly, filthy sluts!' Zehra turned around swiftly and dashed towards the main reception. I followed her. Hands on the waist, huffing and puffing, an angry young man who looked rather too respectable for these shady quarters, was standing by a policeman. He spoke English with an impeccable public school accent. The sloppy cop behind him, whose arms, like those of the Muslim ruler, Allaudin Khilji, reached right down to his knees, was taking long drags at his Ganesh *beedi*. 'Thieves, thieves,' the boy ranted. 'A bunch of ugly whores! I'll have you arrested.'

Noticing me, the young man said: 'Hi,' less to greet me than to seek psychological comfort from someone who, like him, wore a pair of Levi's jeans.

'Hi! Some problem?'

'Yes, I tell you these bitches are all thieves!'

'What's the matter?'

'Oh! Nothing. Something personal.' He sounded a bit embarrassed at being seen around in the 'red light' area.

'The cop's harassing you, is he?'

'No. No. It's these fuckin' whores who are getting too big for their boots! Just you wait and see. I'll sort these…'

'But what happened? You're obviously upset about something.'

He turned towards the *paan*-chewing aunty and threatened her: 'Return my money or I ask the policeman to arrest you.' The enormous middle-aged aunty, indifferent to his threats, responded merely by looking blankly into the blood-shot eyes of the young man. 'Oh *hawaldar sahib!*' she addressed the policeman with an enchanting smile, 'What are you doing in that corner? Come, come, take a seat. What will you have? A cup of tea or something cold?' The policeman promptly walked up, chose the less stained of the two cushioned armchairs as his throne and ordered a chilled Campa-Cola. 'And listen,' the cop told a brothel inmate. 'No ice, please. It's not very safe these days. The other day they found a frozen lizard in an ice-slab!' Finding the conversation drifting from a police complaint to the hazards of using ice in India, the young man said to the policeman: 'Fine, *Hawaldar Sahib*, she won't return my money. We have no choice. Let's lodge a complaint!'

'Well, if you like,' replied the cop, with a late-night yawn. 'You're sure you can't sort this out amicably?'

'No, I want to lodge a formal complaint. The bitches must realise that there is something called the law of the land.'

'OK,' answered the cop, pulling out a set of crumpled brown papers from his plastic briefcase. 'Now what's your name?'

'Rajesh.'

'Rajesh what? Your family name?'

'Rajesh Kumar.'

'Where are you from?'

'Meerut.'

'From Meerut? You don't look like someone from this town.' The fashionable young man looked much too urbane to pass off for a small-town resident. The policeman looked at the man a bit suspiciously, and then, turning the tables on him, asked firmly:

'Are you sure you belong here?'

'From Delhi really.' As the boy answered in a soft murmur, the aunty chuckled teasingly.

'A student, are you?'

'Yeah.'

'Where in Delhi? Which college?'

'Never mind that. Why do you want the name of my college?' The policeman, slurping at his Campa-Cola, reacted rudely: 'Look here, young man, one thing should be clear in your mind. If you have approached the police to register a complaint, you'll have to do it in full compliance with the regulations of the Indian Penal Code. You have to give your address, your profession, and other details. We can't register complaints from nameless ghosts, can we? Do you still want to go ahead with the complaint?'

'Yes.'

'Which college are you from?'

'St. Stephen's College.' The boy looked at me and turned scarlet. He was right, we did have more than jeans in common.

'And now, what's your father's name?'

'What?'

'Your father's name? Yes, you must provide all details.'

'I can't tell you that.'

'Well, if you can't tell me that, I can't file the complaint.' The policeman slapped his file shut and aunty walked out of the room, sniggering and smirking. The policeman lit another *beedi* and asked the boy in seeming confidence:

'But what happened exactly?'

'Well, you know, I went in with a whore and by the time I came out, my wallet had vanished. I'm sure another slut walked in and nicked the wallet from my pants. They're thieves.'

'Now, you see, how can we be certain that it was one of these girls who stole it?' commented the policeman, who, by now, sounded more like the administrative outpost of the brothel than a representative of the Indian state. 'Being an educated man, you know we can't blame anyone in a democracy without a proper witness. If you like, I can still register the complaint but you'll have to give me all the details. How much money was there, anyway?'

'Eight hundred rupees.'

'Gosh! That's an awful lot of money! Why were you carrying so much on you?'

'Never mind why, but I want you to help me recover that money.'

'OK. To help you out, I can mention your father's name as Mr. Kumar. We won't give his initials. What does he do?'

'I can't tell you that.'

'God, this is becoming difficult now. And his address?'

'Come off it, *Hawaldar Sahib*, all this for a small complaint?'

'Then the answer is simple,' asserted the policeman emphatically, 'I can't register this complaint.' The policeman got up angrily, clutching his briefcase in his arm, and walked across to meet aunty. The young man, harassed, turned to me:

'Any ideas? What shall I do?'

'Just give your father's address? They're not going to contact him for a petty complaint like this.'

'One never knows. And I can't put him in the soup for this wretched affair.'

'What does he do? State secret, is it?' I asked amicably.

'He's the Indian Ambassador to a South Asian country.'

'Shit! Drop the whole thing, man.' The young man forgot about the police complaint and started screaming at the top of his voice. 'Whores! Sluts! Thieves! You bitches! You need to be raped by...' Zehra pulled me away: 'Come, let's mind our own business. Aunty will sort it out with the cop. These are everyday affairs here.'

It was late at night. As we walked across the *kotha*, I noticed that the business was past its peak. In contrast to the early evening hours, when the entire place was humming with activity, now the young girls, between twelve and twenty, were standing about in the corridor. Just as I was contemplating that my second opinion of the brothel was not as disgusting as the first, we heard a young girl screaming in pain. 'What's that, Zehra?' Without answering, Zehra led me quickly up the staircase and said: 'Come, we'll sit in my room.'

'But didn't you hear that, Zehra? I think the woman is being raped.'

'You don't understand.'

'But, Zehra, it doesn't take much to understand someone being raped. Can't we go and help her?'

'She is a newcomer to the *kotha*.'

'What do you mean?'

'I'll tell you later. Just follow me into the room.'

The room was a shrine to middle-class taste—posters of actors and actresses on the wall, plastic flowers, a pot of cold water, a chair, a cupboard full of flashy clothes and a low single bed. Zehra took off her sandals and sat up on the bed.

'Who was that girl?' I still couldn't get over the screams.

'She's a newcomer. You see, this is how the girls are brought here. Aunty has a gang of young men working for her. They have contacts in small towns like Gorakhpur, Bairaich, Ballia, all the poor areas of our country. These men approach young girls and lure them with promises of marriage. At times the girls run away themselves, or their parents send them away since they don't have enough even to feed themselves. Some other girls leave thinking they're going to be married into some decent family. That's it. Then they are brought here. The first night, they call it the wedding-night in the brothel jargon, they are raped repeatedly by the pimps who've brought them. Within a few days they understand where they've landed. That's what you heard!'

'And she can't escape?'

'How? Aunty has a private army in this area that can smell a prostitute a mile away. You just can't escape her clutches. This girl you heard screaming will receive clients tomorrow like any other girl at the *kotha*. After a while, she'll get to accept her fate. Even if she wanted to run away, where will she go? She can't go back home, they won't accept her after this profession. She can't go elsewhere, she won't find work. She can't move to another city, nobody will rent her a place. She can't marry, who'd marry her? So you see, this is life.'

Zehra got up and bolted the door from inside. Switching off the top light, she lit a candle and asked me to sit by her side. She looked tired. The gleam in her eyes had somewhat dulled and, ever since our arrival in Meerut, her wit and frothiness had dampened. 'You look a bit shaken,' she remarked. Yes, it was true. The thought of the young girl being raped by her pimp-husband was bad enough but what was worse, with gangsters and cops in her pocket, there wasn't even an escape from the broad-daylight crimes of the unscrupulous aunty.

Zehra was almost asleep when I asked her:

'Tell me, Zehra, did your life begin like this too?'

'Don't be silly,' she said dismissively.

'Why? Doesn't everyone here begin the same way?'

'Yes, but I'm not a prostitute. I am a *tawaiff*. Do you know the difference?'

'Yes, they are the courtesans of the Mughal nobility.'

'Exactly. We are their descendants. I'm one of the few of the sort still left. My mother was the most beautiful *tawaiff* in her youth. No-one could match her looks, dance and song. They say the British administrators and the Nawabs vied with each other to have her for an evening. Now she's withered with age and disease. About to die any day.' Zehra fell asleep on my knee. Her gentle snoring was the first human sound I had heard at the *kotha*.

By the time we got out of the *kotha* the next morning, the city was wide awake. The garbage-women had just swept the streets and specks of dust shone in the morning sun. The milkmen, with large steel cans tied around their bicycles, were on their way home.

At Ghanta Ghar, we caught a glimpse of the policeman we had met the night before but, as Zehra explained, it was an unwritten rule of her trade that you never greeted a visitor to the *kotha* in public. Sighting an unoccupied rickshaw, we hopped onto it and Zehra promptly ordered him to take us to her house.

'So you saw what a *kotha* looks like?'

'Yes.'

'Not too shocked, I hope?'

'Well. So far I had only read about it in books. It's far worse in real life.'

'And thanks to me you got to see it. No ordinary person can even enter the place,' she boasted.

'And you? Aunty lets you go scot-free?'

'Why not? The place runs on my name. I'm the most solicited singer and dancer in these parts. It helps when you're a reputed *tawaiff* and then, I am a *khandani*, a lineage *tawaiff*.' Zehra nudged me gently with her elbow and said with childlike perkiness: 'So you see, you are with the queen of Meerut!' The rickshaw-puller must have been sneaking on our conversation, for he looked back and tittered unconsciously. Zehra whispered: 'Shsh! I shouldn't be talking that loud. They recognize me here…'

Zehra's house was modest. Dimly lit, humid, plaster flaking off the walls, the entire building seemed to be collapsing under the weight of history and time. As we entered the staircase, a well-fed rat, the size of a mongoose, sat obstinately on a step gazing at us in benign indifference. 'Scared of rats, are you?' asked Zehra. 'Neither rats nor ghosts!' Zehra smiled tenderly, took my hand and led me up the steps with the sole warning that her mother was seriously ill and I should refrain from making her talk too much.

We walked right round the *parchchatti*, a rectangular balcony overlooking the inner courtyard. Such balconies, deprived of any view of the outside world, were first conceived by the Rajputs and the Muslims. In many ways they were the architectural equivalents of the *purdah*; just as the women did not have the right to face men in public, the top-floor *parchchattis* ensured that women would not meet the men-visitors in private too. That Zehra and her mother, both *tawaiffs*, lived in such a building was obviously less by choice than by sheer compulsion of finding a cheap lodging.

'*Amma? Ma!*' Zehra walked into her mother's room and said: '*Adab, ma.* Meet a friend. He's a writer.'

'*Adabarzhai beta.* Please make yourself comfortable. So you write. How nice! My husband is a poet, too.' Turning towards Zehra, she asked: 'Did it go well at the Tikadevi *mela*? You took long. Anyway, call your father.'

'What will you drink? Hot or cold?' she asked me, sitting up in bed.

'Please don't get up,' I said to Zehra's mother. 'Zehra told me you've not been keeping well.'

'Yes, that's true. The doctor's say there's little hope.'

'Come, come. I'm sure you'll get well soon.'

'No, my son, don't say that,' she said, imploringly, 'now you should just wish that death comes early. It's very painful. I'm just waiting for the orders from Allah...'

Zehra's father entered and greeted me with a bow reminiscent of the profound art of Mughal courtesy. From the very first word he uttered in Urdu, poetry flowed. His metaphors, his lyricism and his choice of words carried the stamp of human grace. Taking me to another room, he said: 'So you're from Paris, Zehra told me. What a great city! Rimbaud, Baudelaire, Sartre, Camus! Great culture!'

'Have you read them in English?'

'Yes, but my English is not very good. I've read translations in Urdu. You don't need to read all of Rimbaud to realise what a great poet he was. What a shame you are here at a wrong time! I would have loved to invite you to a poetry-reading festival…'

'Yes, I learnt *ma* is not well.'

'Well, she'll be another victim of history. Another martyr at the hands of fanaticism.'

'Of fanaticism? I thought she was ill.'

'No, no. Her story is no longer a secret in these parts. Years ago, we lived in Moradabad. She was stabbed in a communal riot by a Muslim fanatic. You see, she is a Hindu by birth and I, a Muslim. People around us didn't like the fact that we'd got married. So when the fires of fanaticism erupted one day, one of her own cousins came and stabbed her. After that day, she's been in and out of hospitals.'

'But what really…'

'Please, let's drop the subject. It's a sad story heading towards its end.'

Zehra barged in through the curtain, looking oddly excited in a household where the spectre of death loomed large. Behind Zehra, hidden behind the curtain, was another girl whose tiny feet and blue slippers peeked out from the bottom.

'Meet my sister, Nishant,' said Zehra before turning to her sister. 'Come *appa*, don't be shy, come on in.' Zehra raised the curtain and the young girl walked in.

'Her name is Shabnam,' said Zehra proudly.

'Oh! Shabnam?'

'Oh! *Bhaijaan?* Gangotri!…' She murmured in silent recognition.

Mandakini

JAYA, SMITA, ZEHRA. SMITA, ZEHRA, JAYA. ZEHRA, JAYA, Smita. Each resembles the other. Jaya sees herself in the mirror, the mirror shows Zehra. Smita sees herself in the mirror, she sees Jaya. Zehra's embraces echo the pain of Jaya's autumns. Jaya's fragrance shines in the tears of Zehra's partings. Zehra arrives merely to announce the way Jaya had left. She arrives, and as she arrives, she is also disappearing. She disappears only to arrive on the doorstep of another surprise. Yet no-one ever comes or leaves. Life is a passage, Ganga tells me, between the endless corridors of absence and presence. Life is a circle of little mirrors, mirrors of absence and presence, that Ganga herself has described around the solitude of the human soul. Come, my pilgrim, says Ganga, I will show you that *sanjog* and *viyog*, union and separation, are written in the book of the invisible heavens. Come, my seeker, I will lend you the eye to unravel the invisible. Come, my worshipper, I will lend you the colour of my almond eyes. Come, follow me, follow me silently on my passage to infinity and look inwards, deep within you, where I flow serenely along the windpipe of your soul.

Having said that, she curved right and disappeared behind the veil of green trees where *sanyasis* befriend the deers to re-enact the beginnings of history.

If Ganga had offered Zehra, as that gift of union and disunion that completes the cycle of life, she also gave the strength to overcome the blue wound of a love that never was and that shall never be. Ganga is a healer, magical and modest. Where she heals, no-one shall ever know and how she heals, none shall ever know. She just heals, making you drink a heady potion from her eyes, which, the more you consume, the more you find yourself transported beyond your mortal pain. For forget not the passing pilgrim of my waters, said Ganga, your wounds are mortal but my touch immortal. Immortal she has been and immortal she shall be...

Ganga heals only when her seeker has become a part of her and she of him. It is not the silence of her waters that heals, nor its rhythm, nor the lapping of her waves because, even for her, healing is not just magic, but magic as active therapy. She weaves around her pilgrim a spectacle of purity, she offers him a feel of the glass-heavens where she belongs, and the seeker must accept the penance to experience this spectacle. Her limitless skies, the plopping sound of dolphins, the chirping of sparrows, the demented laws of her geometry, the contrasts in her landscape, the rhythm of her liquid eyes, her cliffs, her sand, her colour, create that spectacle of purity which alone can inspire an inner silence or light, where transcendence of the mortal becomes possible. The holy dip in Ganga, therefore, is not a bath to heal wounds or to wash away sins, but just one milestone of a long journey of self-consciousness which could dissolve wounds or make *moksha* possible. Ganga is the blue-name of a mirror, which the more honestly you face, the more it reflects, and the more dishonestly you hold, the more it distorts. 'My mirror smashed, like a burst of laughter'- was that Apollinaire strolling with Jaya on the banks of Ganga?

Since my return from Meerut, we had been on the boat the whole morning. The rowing was smooth. The draught in the river had gradually increased and from the very sound of the oars it was clear that it was not in her depths that Ganga would betray us anymore. For some mysterious reason that went beyond the tips of money, Ram and Peer Singh seemed to have forgiven me for my amorous heresies. Warmth and friendship replaced reproach, and it was perhaps because of the new mood that they now chose to call me 'bhaiya' rather than 'sahib'.

We now had a new passenger on board. A young, bespectacled, pock-marked man called Govind Narain Chatturvedi who, as the boatmen explained to me, was on his way to the same village, Narora, which was also our destination for the day. 'Comrade', as he liked to be called, was a real bookworm, reminiscent of the studious boys at school. For the two hours that we had spent on the boat, he hadn't uttered a single word. Comrade was lost in his world of thoughts and strategies, with his head plunged into a Hindi translation of Lenin's *What is to be done?* It was as if a revolution awaited him on the far bank of Ganga.

'Bhaiya, bhaiya,' exclaimed Ram, 'look, look!' A dead body, draped in a white sheet, had suddenly risen to the surface. It floated lazily, like someone basking in the sun. Since the beginning of our journey a few days ago, there had been no dearth of floating corpses, often decomposed and bloated. Every Indian who has known the banks of Ganga is aware that the village poor often leave their dead to the unfathomable depths of the sacred goddess. In this tragic scenario on the 'untouchables' of the Gangetic plains, the poor man not only lacks the resources to keep his family alive, he also lacks them to cremate his dead with dignity. The sight of this white body, however, was particularly eerie. Its shroud looked new and in its overall contours and shape, it seemed fresh and youthful. In all likelihood, it had been recently immersed in the water, with the help of heavy stones. The weights had got loosened, and the body was ejected to the surface.

Two dogs jumped into the river and started heading excitedly towards the body. With the perfection of trained police dogs, they held the body at two ends and pulled it slowly onto the bank. Once on the bank, the dogs became nervous – or scared. They stood at a distance and barked. They approached the body, then retreated hastily, and barked again. The dogs hovered around the body for a while. Testing for life? Scared of crime? Ghosts? Act of natural sadism? Then, one of the dogs slowly mustered up the courage to go closer. He snapped at the white sheet with his paw and retreated. Encouraged, the other dog came up and snapped at the sheet with his teeth, and withdrew hastily. The test was over. The body didn't react. The dogs pounced on the corpse, lending this sinister sight a touch of sport.

'But what are the dogs doing in our ancestral domain?' asked a vulture. Within seconds, five vultures descended on the bank. The dogs barked at the vultures: *'Ne touche pas à ma proie!'* The vultures retorted in the same words, 'Don't you touch my prey!' The dogs barking and the vultures flapping their wings, the fight continued until ten more vultures, smelling the white sheet as the 'muleta', alighted on the bank. The two teams were finely balanced. The match began. The dogs fought the vultures and the vultures, dogs. First round: Quits! Second round: Quits! The body waited silently with the only question on its lips: Will Ganga deliver me to the heavens? As Ganga withheld her verdict, the vultures and the dogs struck a hasty compromise.

Dividing the melon, they jointly pulled apart the human flesh. Within fifteen minutes, the two species had resolved the eternal riddle of how a human body becomes a fearsome ghost... The skeleton, with its right arm raised vertically, seemed to bid us farewell when I exclaimed with disgust:

'What a ghastly sight!'

'No, *bhaiya*,' said Ram, 'this is quite normal.'

'Dreadful.'

'No, *bhaiya*, this is common.'

'Common or not Ram,' remarked Govind-the-Comrade, taking time off from Lenin, 'it is sad that the poor chap didn't even have money for a proper cremation. In Hinduism, everyone has the right to a decent cremation.'

'You're probably right, *babuji*, but who has the money for cremation these days? The wood itself costs four hundred rupees! So they bring the body to the banks. As far as I know, barely thirty out of a hundred bodies get cremated. The rest are dropped into the river. The poor man…'

'No, *bhaiya*,' Peer Singh interrupted Ram, 'these bodies don't only belong to the poor, a lot of them are actually victims of criminals. There are fights over money and land, and the murdered are just dropped into the river at night. By the time the bodies surface they are so badly decomposed that no-one can tell who was who. But *bhaiya*, Gangaji is an entire universe unto herself. She has piety, she has crime, she has love, she has hatred. She has everything. She is the river of life.'

'Tell me, Peer,' I asked, 'we've seen so many bodies on Ganga until now. Doesn't it bother the bathers? Doesn't it hurt their sensibilities?'

'No, *bhaiya*, not at all. What's in a body! The spirit has already escaped it. Heaven or hell, wherever it's destined to go, it's gone. So what's left? The body is a mere cover for our souls. Yes, sacred texts consider cremation to be the appropriate farewell ritual, but leaving them to Gangaji is equally holy. Her waters have great qualities, *bhaiya*. She can cure all, can heal everything, she can bestow peace on the most tortured soul. Nobody objects to bodies in Ganga because she is life and, then, she has the power to purify everything.'

Peer Singh picked up the wooden mast we had on board,

and plunged it into the water to measure the depth. 'Oh! It's quite deep! Drop the oars, Ram, let her go with the wind.' As the boat cruised smoothly, pushed by an eastward breeze, Peer Singh opened his cloth bag and pulled out an old silver box. 'Will you have *paan, bhaiya?*' The studious Lenin-reader looked up and expressed his desire to have a betel-leaf with a good dose of lime-stone paste. Peer Singh took four yellowish betel-leaves, washed them, put some *katha* and *choona* paste, added areca nut, cardamom and some potent raw tobacco for a nice and high feel. Soon the tobacco began to work and Ganga, which was getting hotter and sweatier, began to feel light and pleasant.

I had just about managed to draw Comrade into a discussion when Ram, still preoccupied with the mystical properties of Ganga, remarked wondrously: '*Bhaiya*, Ganga*ji* can do amazing things. Even we didn't believe stories about Ganga but, slowly, one had to admit things we saw with our own eyes. Once, a young boy was bitten by a snake. He was immediately covered with cow-dung because cow-dung can often heal fresh snake-bites. Anyway, it didn't work and the boy died. The family shaved his scalp and took the body to the banks of Ganga*ji* to perform the last rites. The moment some Ganga*jal* was sprinkled on him, the boy came alive. We all saw it! Now, you see…'

'But Ram,' asked Comrade, irascibly, 'had he died in the first place?'

'Yes.'

'Did you see it with your eyes? Otherwise, there is many a quack in our villages who often declares a healthy man dead!'

'No, *sahib*. He was dead. He didn't breathe. He was as white as snow. He had died. Even his grandfather agreed that the boy had died. You don't believe me? Let me tell you another story. My father was a witness to the whole episode. Before the Partition of India in 1947, there was a girl who was bitten by a cobra in the fields. She was found dead. The family was poor, so they brought her to Ganga and immersed her in the waters. A few days later, a Muslim walking on the banks downstream heard a girl crying. This young girl was obviously not dead. He brought her up. Then came the Partition of India and the Muslim gentleman chose to settle down in Pakistan. The girl went with him and grew up in Pakistan. After many years, the girl was told the story of her childhood. She wanted to return to her village. Her father brought her over. The entire village gathered to meet her.'

'Where's the woman now, Ram?'

'Back in Pakistan. The villagers allowed her to go back. She had a Muslim name, a Muslim life-style. There was no point keeping her back.'

'Did you meet the woman yourself?' asked Comrade sceptically.

'I told you. My father told me the story.'

'Enough of this, Ram' asserted Comrade, dismissively, 'you uneducated village folk would believe anything. In my own village, they relate a hilarious story. One day two young girls were declared dead and immersed in Gangaji. The next morning, one of the two girls became alive. Now, both the families in the village claimed that she was their dead daughter and both asserted that their daughter was sent back alive because they were Ganga-worshippers. The result was that the families fought with each other. There was bloodshed. Two young men died! Ridiculous! This is the sad world of your superstitions, Ram.'

'No, *sahib*. My story is one hundred percent true. I hear they are even going to make a film on this.'

'Oh! These wretched filmwalas!' lamented Comrade. 'They make films because you believe their tales, and they believe you because you make their films possible. Between superstitions, ghosts and this stupid cinema, this country will go to dogs!'

'No, *sahib*,' Ram persisted, 'you've been to school, you're educated, you are our master. We know you don't believe such things. But Gangaji has incredible properties. We bow before the might of this great goddess. After all, *sahib*, there are so many rivers in our country, but why is it that it is only Gangaji who commands such respect?'

Ram's naive interrogation and deep belief managed to set Comrade thinking. 'That's an interesting question', remarked Comrade Govind Narain Chatturvedi, setting aside his copy of Lenin and hastily scribbling a few notes in his scrawl-book. He cleared his throat and spoke pedantically:

'Interesting question! Wish the answer was that simple! You see Ram, to know answers to such questions, you need to know the history of our civilisation, the history of India, the significance of Ganga in our history. A long time ago...'

'We don't know much about history and politics, *sahib*. Our question is quite simple. There are so many rivers in our country. Why just one Ganga? Why one river-goddess?'

'You need to know Ganga's history to answer this question. Do you know who the Aryans were?'

'What do you mean were, they are. We are Aryans!'

'Well, the Aryans came to this land some 1,500 years before Christ...'

'Before who?'

'Jesus Christ. *Isaah Masi.*'

'But what do Christians have to do with Gangaji?' Ram looked perplexed.

'Because it's the Christian calendar we use nowadays! Anyway, that's immaterial. The Aryans came a long time ago. When they arrived from the west, for a while they moved about in areas like the Punjab, looking for hospitable terrain to settle down. Until then, they had been living on the produce of cattle. Now, the first prospect of proper cultivation came up only when they reached the banks of Ganga. The soil was fertile. The forests provided wood for constructing huts and making agricultural tools. The terrain was flat, good for cultivation. This first contact with Ganga, therefore, was the most significant to our civilisation. Not only did the waters of Ganga made life and cultivation easy, it also made transportation possible...'

'Yes, they say in the ancient texts that our ancestors had big ships and spacecraft, well before the Americans made them,' reflected Ram, trying to sound scholarly.

'We'll come to that later, but what is important to understand is the central position occupied by the river Ganga during the first phase of our history. It was through Ganga that the Aryans established other cities. They began close to Hastinapur, and migrated further and further towards the east. Kaushambi and Kashi, the first big cities of the Aryan history, were all built on the banks of Ganga. After the cities were established, other things followed. When people began to lead settled lives, there was more production of 'artisanal' goods. That, in turn, created trade. Again, Ganga became the main channel for the exchange of goods. So Ganga, the first river which came on the way of the incoming Aryans, became the very life and soul of a new civilisation. With cities and the first governments...'

'You mean these governments and politicians were there even at that time?' Ram laughed aloud.

'Don't laugh, please! Let me explain. With the kings, the princes and the whole state around them, a new society started to take shape. In fact, Ganga was so important those days that virtually all the major battles of that time were fought to gain control of lucrative spots on the banks of the river. Then, Ganga became the inspiration for so many other things. *Vedas*, *Puranas*,

Sastras, were all conceived on the banks of Ganga. So Ganga became such an immense source of life and imagination that she became the subject of all forms of fantasy. She became a goddess and...'

'You mean she was not a goddess!' Ram cried in protest.

'Wait a minute, *bhaiya,*' said Comrade, with the patronizing gentleness of a school-teacher, 'Ganga was given the status of goddess by man. Over the course of centuries, the future generations came to actually believe that she was a goddess! That's how myths are born.'

'What's born?'

'Myth. A myth is a long beautiful story that sounds as true as real.'

'You mean Gangaji is not a goddess. Strange is the world of you educated men!'

'Not just a goddess, Ganga became everything. She fired the imagination of everyone. This is proved by the different names given to Ganga. For instance, Ganga is called *Vishnu-padmajasambhuta,* she who emerged from the lotus foot of Vishnu. This is obviously a name created by some religious writer. Look at another name, *Bahi-ksira,* a cow which gives milk. Some cow herder might have named her thus. So many names. A poet named her Mandakini, she who flowed calmly, a mystic called her *Trilokapathagamini* she who traversed the three universes, a musician named her *Sugosha,* the melodious. So you see Ganga became whatever one wished her to be. It is a myth. Like the Hindu gods and goddesses...'

'You mean *Bhagwan* Ram, Krishna, *Sitamaiya,* Shiv, Vishnu did not exist?' Ram sounded offended.

'No. They're all mythical heroes.'

'What! They didn't exist.'

'Not in history at least.'

'You mean sixty crore Hindus in India who believe this are all crazy!'

'I don't know about that. But in history, there were no Shivas and Vishnus.'

'*Vah!*' said Ram, in half-anger, half-sarcasm, 'you seem to be the only *guru* in the world. Sixty crore minds are wrong and only Comrade Govind Narain Chatturvedi is right. You really don't believe that Lord Ram and *Sitamaiya* existed? All these stories are false?'

'Not false but imaginary. In any case, history has no proof of this.'

'Funny man! Who needs proof when people are the proof. People know they are gods, isn't that proof enough? You mean Lord Rama didn't go to Lanka for exile, that he didn't defeat Ravana-the-demon?'

'History is not clear about Rama. Some say he was a small tribal king. *Ramayana* is a story woven around his life.'

'*Vah!* Chatturvedi *sahib!* Never seen a Brahmin like you! You call Ram and Sita fake, you don't believe in our gods and religion...'

'A great man once said that religion is the opium of the people.' Comrade Chatturvedi seemed to have started a regular study circle with the poor boatmen.

'Why is religion opium?' queried Ram.

'Because opium is bad for the mind. It intoxicates man to the point of ruining himself. All intoxication is bad.'

'What's wrong with intoxication?' argued Peer Singh, who so far had chosen to be an observer to the discussion. Peer Singh probably felt offended because he had proudly admitted on the first day of our journey that he was an avid consumer of opium. Comrade reflected for a while before saying:

'Why is intoxication bad! Because, because... funny man!

Because it ruins your health.'

'But anything can ruin one's health. Too much milk gives dysentery. Too much of rice produces gas. Too much *ghee* is bad for the heart. Have you ever tried opium?'

'Good heavens, no! It's not good for you.'

'How can you say that?' Peer Singh was beginning to lose his patience.

'Strange people! This is nothing new. Everyone knows that opium kills man.'

'Why? You've never tried it.'

'People say so.'

'And so?'

'My grandfather died of opium... Strange! This is the first time I've met someone who is defending opium addiction. I see hundreds around me who say opium is bad. Shall I believe them or you?'

'*Vah* Comrade! You see sixty crore people worshipping a god, but you still don't believe their divinity exists. Here, you haven't even tried opium, and you think it kills man. Before denouncing opium, Comrade *sahib*, you should try it like your grandfather. Who knows, maybe he died a happy man.'

Star

'HELLO, HELLO, CAN YOU HEAR ME? HELLO! BOOKING?'
'Stop screaming!' the telephone man snarled at me. 'What do you want?'

'Sorry, I thought you couldn't hear me. Is that '180' Trunks Booking, please?'

'No. This is '199' Assistance. Call '180' for Bookings.'

I dialled again.

'Hello, is that '180' Bookings please?'

'*Are baba*, this is Assistance,' he answered curtly.

'I think I just spoke to you, sir. Sorry to bother you. I can't get through to the Trunks operator. Can you...'

'Yes, I can see that. But this is Assistance here.'

'Well, could you please assist me get through to '180'? I have an urgent call for Delhi.'

'Delhi or Calcutta, that is not our business, sir. How can I explain to you? You are at Assistance, not Bookings.'

'Can you help me get Booking?' I pleaded.

'We can't get you numbers within the exchange itself.'

'But I can't get through. I've an urgent call.'

'I can't do much about it, sir, try again.' He slammed the phone down.

I thought of calling the Telephone Exchange supervisor.

'Hello. 43217, supervisor.'

'Who?'

'Telephone supervisor?'

'No, Divisional Commissioner's residence.' I dialled again.

'Is this the...'

'Oh, the same Johnny again! Stop disturbing us every now and then! I've told you this is the Commissioner's residence. And don't dial again. There's an important election meeting going on.' I tried '180' again.

'Hello, Assistance?'

'Yes, may I help you?' someone answered with unusual politeness.

'Can you help me, sir? I've been trying...'

'Yes, yes, we're here to help you. Tell me, where's the fire?'

'What fire?'

'Quick! Give me the address please. The fire brigade will be there in a minute.'

'Sorry.' Fed up, I put the phone down. One last try at the Trunks supervisor's number.

'Hello! supervisor?'

'Yes, supervisor.'

'Trunk calls supervisor?'

'Yes, yes, Trunks supervisor.'

'Good afternoon, sir.' He greeted me courteously.

'Good afternoon. I've been trying to place a 'lightning' call through to Delhi since this morning.'

'Really, so have I!'

'What ! Aren't you the Trunks supervisor?'

'Hell! I think we've got caught in a cross-connection. I thought you were the supervisor. I too have been trying since this morning. Well, you know what Allahabad phones are like. Good luck.'

I was stuck in Allahabad. For three days, I had searched desperately for two boatmen willing to row me down to Benares.

Some were scared of the unknown, others feared criminals. The situation was so hopeless that, in one case, a boatman turned down my offer to pay him 3000 rupees for a three-day journey. One other boatman, old and drooping, was half-willing to consider my tempting offer but only on condition that two armed escorts from the district police could be asked to come on board. On a journey which, by now, had begun to resemble the military expeditions of the nineteenth century, the best suggestion came from my friend, Sanjay, now posted to Allahabad as a senior officer of the district administration. Sanjay had found out that the flood-relief department of Allahabad owned two motor boats which, given official permission, could be asked to take me down to Benares. The authorisation to use them, however, could only come from the virtually inaccessible District Magistrate. Since 'DM' *sahib* would not entertain requests from non-entities like me, it was imperative that someone higher than him in the *durbars* of Delhi should call in my support, for otherwise, there was a good chance that my Ganga would end in Allahabad.

I tried the phone again. Dead as a log. Furious with Indian telephones, I complained to Sanjay:

'Your bloody phones are horrid!'

'It's not our phones.' Sanjay retorted sarcastically, 'It's you bloody French who've dumped obsolete exchanges here! The Third World has become a gutter for the multi-nationals... But hang on a sec, let me ask one of our chaps to keep trying the number.' Sanjay pressed on the buzzer to call one of his peons.

Ram Lal, dark, betel-stained and corpulent, like three big watermelons piled on top of each other, entered with a worried look on his face. 'Yes, *sahib*,' he muttered.

'Come on, stand straight. Why are you huffing and puffing like a steam-engine? Haven't had a heart-attack, have you?' Sanjay quipped, in a tone of harmless authority.

'A bright guy. I like him in his earlier films more, though. He comes through as a very intelligent chap.'

'Stop being a pseudo, you hypocrite! But what about his looks? Tall, handsome, strong, rich, what else do you want in life, honey?' She laughed hysterically, as if undressing herself on the telephone.

'You sound pretty turned on, don't you? Well, I find him quite intelligent. I met him the other day you know.'

'What? Met him! Where?'

'He'd come to meet the officials on election duty.'

'And you talked to him?'

'Said hello, that's about all. He came in a politician's outfit. In a white *pyjama-kurta*. I tell you he didn't look glamorous at all.'

'And you didn't talk to him?'

'In front of all the District Commissioners and the rest? You must be joking. It's a different world in civil administration.'

'To hell with your administration! Tell me, is he going to come again to one of these meetings?'

'Not that I've heard of.'

'*Hai*, I'd love to meet him.'

'But hasn't he come to meet the *army-walas* as yet?'

'What chance! He won't come to our wretched barracks!'

'Gosh! You're crazy about him, aren't you, Radha?'

'The whole world is! Not just me. I tell you, if he wins, it's because he can charm the *saris* off women.'

'Shut up, will you? Are you drunk?'

'Yes, on A-mi-tabh. Oh! He turns me on.'

'Your husband can probably hear you speak.'

'Not to worry! He's far away with his Generals in Delhi.'

'Are you going to the election meeting tonight?'

'Where?'

'You didn't know? Amitabh is speaking at K.P. College.'

'What?'
'Yeah! This evening.'
'I didn't know that. *Pucca*, I'll go.'
'All alone?'
'Why not?'
'But there'll be a *hujjar* crowd there. Aren't you scared?'
'I can sit in the car and watch.'
'Rajiv Gandhi is coming too.'
'Don't say that. Two handsome men in one evening.'
'Just shut up, Radha. You'll get me into trouble. I'm putting the phone down.'
'How you've changed since college days, Mala!'

The giddy telephone conversation ended, but it had aroused my curiosity about the meeting. Leaving Sanjay to deal with Delhi, I set off to explore the cinematic ambience on the banks of Ganga. I hired a rickshaw and headed straight for the K.P. College grounds.

'Are you in the film-vilm world, *sahib?*' asked the rickshaw-puller.

'No, no, I have nothing to do with cinema.'

'But you're going to Amitabh's meeting, aren't you?'

'Yes, like so many others.'

'I'm sure you're here for some shooting.' he insisted.

'Not at all. What makes you think that?'

'Oh yes, *sahib*,' he said in his Bhojpuri accent, 'your jacket, your camera, your white shoes, they're all so filmy!' He couldn't have embarrassed my poor Adidas shoes more.

'No, no. I assure you I'm just a visitor in Allahabad.'

'There's no one who can stop him from winning. We'll make sure he wins.' Lively, gay and boisterous, the young bronze-skinned rickshaw-puller began to sing aloud what seemed to be an Amitabh campaign song.

> 'Hey, listen carefully my friends,
> Amitabh is here among us today.
> Listen carefully, my friends,
> We owe him for the fun
> He's given us over years
> One vote for his songs,
> Another for his fights,
> Another for his tears,
> Another for his smile...
> Listen, listen, my friends,
> Amitabh is here among us today.
> Win he must for lose a hero can never...

The grounds of K.P. College were overflowing. People everywhere–on cars, on buses, on trucks, on walls, on bicycles, on trees, on rooftops. The meeting resembled an enormous festival of cinephiles. Nothing defined the face of this crowd. It wore all colours, it contained all ages, it spoke all dialects of the region, it carried the stamp of all classes, castes and religions. If it shared anything in common, it was a peculiar curiosity, that hypnotised look in the eye, when a long repressed dream is about to burst into flames of reality. Suddenly, someone in the crowd, cried out: 'Amitabh has arrived...'

A white Fiat was mobbed. Within seconds, the car had transformed into a wonder-toy, surrounded by concentric circles of hysteria, delirium and rippling smiles. Young sixteen-year-olds caressed the gently advancing tinted windshield, as if touching the face of the star. Soon, it was difficult for the car to advance any further. The security men jumped out to throw a cordon against the frenzied crowd. Finding it unmanageable, the police started a lathi charge. The cinephiles retaliated with slogans against the police. Bachchan, in his new role as politician, jumped out of the car and motioned to the cops to show restraint. The crowd responded to Amitabh's gesture with a chorus: 'Long live Amitabh! Victory to Amitabh...'

The crowd ogled, as Amitabh and his relatives walked towards the stage. Despite Bachchan's best efforts to leave his film image behind in Bombay, the crowd could hardly believe that his entourage of young women had not followed him on his electoral trail. As the Congress party activists, half-suspected by the crowd to be a bunch of Bombay actors and actresses in Gandhian costumes, advanced towards the podium, one of them, an old woman, presumably one of Amitabh's relatives, hastened to pull the edge of her *sari* over her face. Finding her face become evasive, a fan screamed: 'Oh! Oh! Oh! Rekha! Rekha! The glamour-girl! Amitabh's girl!' There was a virtual stampede until the old woman chose to throw the veil off her face and thundered: 'I'm not Rekha, my sons. I am your grandmother!'

A rotund pretentious organiser took the microphone and announced: 'Shri Amitabh Bachchan is among us. Shri Bachchan needs no introduction but...' The crowd heckled him out, shouting in unison, 'We want Amitabh! Amitabh! Amitabh!' The spotlight moved on to Amitabh's face. The face was lit up by a flood of lights; behind him, the glow of the twilight-hour, the hour of magic, the hour of hypnosis. Master of his craft, Amitabh first chose to stand motionless, statuesque, hands folded. The crowd fell silent, waiting for the hero to disclose what next. And, in a flash, Amitabh broke into a full smile. Recognizing in that magical smile a glimpse of his films, the crowd went berserk. It was like Julius Caesar being applauded for his victories.

Bachchan began his speech. He was short and precise. 'You've seen me before. That was an artificial Amitabh. Artificial screen, fake costumes, fake make-up, fake stories. What you see before you now is the genuine Amitabh, the Amitabh of your land, the

Allahabad boy back in his hometown...' The crowd cheered and, taking the cue from the hysterical crowds, the star announced: 'My opponent has slandered me for working in films. He has said obscene and vulgar things. I would not do the same to him. My opponent is my elder. I respect his seniority. My upbringing has taught me to never be disrespectful to elders...'

That was it. The good old moralist image of the superstar was complete. Just as he had been accepted on the screen, he was once again accepted by his audience in the theatre of live performances. Amitabh asked: 'Those who will vote for the Congress, raise your hands.' 200,000 hands went up in the air. Those who will vote for Rajiv Gandhi, raise the other hand too.' 400,000 hands went up in the air. The crowd and Amitabh, their hands raised in homage to the cinematic memory of the assassinated Indira Gandhi, stood silent, upright and resolute. Amitabh appeared to be the Pope, Mussolini, Hitler or Lenin. His popularity was frightening and that of cinema even more...

The mass hysteria had exhausted me mentally. Slightly pensive, I strolled down to a wayside tea-stall and ordered a glass of tea. An elderly villager, clad in a white *dhoti* and a loose hand-spun *kurta*, came and sat at my table. His unusually long, chiselled moustache reminded me of the Rajput warriors in eighteenth century miniatures. Arching his eyebrows, he asked me:

'You came for the meeting?'

'Yes.'

'Oh you youngsters! You'll all be ruined by cinema one day!' The old man's sharp comment didn't really upset me for, in these parts of the country, most elderly people speak with unquestionable patriarchal authority.

'Why do you say that? You are an opposition supporter, are you?'

'No, no, far from it. I didn't come for the meeting. I'm

from a nearby village, Karchchana. My grandson studies at the University here. He hadn't written home for quite some time, so I came by to see him. I went to his room but he wasn't in. His neighbour said that he had gone for this actor's meeting. Oh these young boys! I'm fed up. He's flunked three times in his exams. And the idiot is going to fail again! Each time you see him, he wants more money. For books, fees, paper, pencil–his lists are endless. And when you come here to see what he is up to, they say he has gone to Amitabh's meeting... The world has changed.' He sounded perturbed.

'Your boy is young, *tauji*,' I said, trying to calm him down, 'some fun at this age is his right, isn't it?

'No! His bloody job is to study, otherwise he can come and till the land in the village. This cinema will destroy him.'

'But everyone watches cinema, not just your grandson.'

'Well, then, cinema will destroy everyone. If I find my grandson this evening, I'm going to ask him to pack up and return to the village with me.'

The teen-aged waiter brought a glass of hot tea for the old man. He took one sip and screamed at the young boy:

'This is not tea, it is horse-piss. Put some more milk in this glass. Bloody thieves, these restaurant-*walas*! They cheat even on a glass of tea!' The old man removed his shoes and sat cross legged on the bench.

'But what do you have against cinema and your grandson going to one of Bachchan's meetings?' I asked the old man who, having shouted at the waiter, seemed to have recovered his calm.

'You're young, my son. You perhaps don't know much about the great history of our country. I myself was in politics for over fifty years. I've seen Mahatma Gandhi, Nehru, Jaiprakash, Indira, everyone. Tell me, this actor, what does he know about politics and our country? He has no programme! No projects!

No vision! Nothing! Could a man like him ever stand next to Pandit Nehru on the same platform? Never. It was a different epoch. There was some sincerity about politics. Now this young boy knows he can pull in votes because of cinema, so he quit cinema and moved into politics. Can you imagine the effect of these mammoth meetings on the mind of this actor?'

'What?'

'It's obvious he thinks his cinema can buy anything: money, votes, women. He must be intoxicated with power even before he has seen the face of the parliament. Cinema is a poison, my son. I don't mind song, dance, drama. They're fun. But cinema gives a strange power to those who make it. It has the capacity to turn an actor into a god. Look at this actor in the elections, he is like a god. He's not fighting elections, he's shooting another film... Then, most of this cinema is immoral. It has destroyed our religion, our lifestyle. It has spun the heads of our youth.' The old man had not quite finished when two young short-haired university girls, elegantly dressed, got off their bicycles and confidently ordered two glasses of tea. The old man leaned towards me and confided in his husky voice: 'Worse, cinema has destroyed our women.'

'Why?'

'Fashion! Every girl in the city today wants to be a heroine. A girl has long hair today and tomorrow her hair is the length of my grandson's! If this goes on any longer, a husband won't recognize his wife the next morning... Oh, the times have changed!'

Two young men got off a scooter and joined the university girls at their table. As they began giggling, laughing and discussing the Amitabh meeting they had been to, the old man nudged me with his elbow and said:

'Just look at that! Look at the way they're talking. They're not women, these shameless creatures. Look at the way they're talking about this actor! Oh! This nation will go to dogs.' The grandfatherly defender of the traditional order then put on his spectacles, stared one last time at one of the two girls and astonished, asked me: ' Is that a cigarette in her hand? Oh God! What has the world come to?' Scandalised, the man slipped on his sandals and took the road which, presumably, led to his grandson's university hostel.

Back at Sanjay's house, I was informed that the call to Delhi had come through, and that someone high-up in the Ministry of Home Affairs had spoken to the Divisional Commissioner asking him to lend me a boat and a two-man crew for a journey up to Benares. Sanjay agreed to accompany me on Ganga for a day or two. Since we planned to leave early next morning for the *ghats,* we had a quick dinner. Vidyun, Sanjay's wife, led me to the guest room overlooking a garden. After weeks on Ganga, the sight of a bed, spotless bed-sheets and clean toilets was paradise. As I got into the bed, I noticed a large poster on the front wall: a man in baggy black clothes, a moustache, a hat and a cane. Saying goodnight to Charlie Chaplin, I turned off the lights.

Panda

I WAS FAST ASLEEP. SOMEBODY KNOCKED AT THE DOOR. The door that opened onto the lawns.

'Who's it?'

'It's me, *sahib*.'

'Who!'

'Ram Lal, *sahib*.' Ram Lal? Had he come to repair another telephone? Recognizing his voice, I opened the door.

'What's it? What time is it?'

'Four o'clock, *sahib*.'

'What's it?'

'A telegram, *sahib*,' he muttered grimly. A telegram in semi-rural India conjures up images of a calamity.

'Shall I wake up Sanjay then?

'No, *sahib*. It's for you.'

'For me?' I was surprised. Handing over the telegram, he retreated.

'*Reaching Benares thirty-first December. Rendezvous Dasaswamedha Ghat the hour of sunset love Jaya.*'

If I had offered everything that Jaya ever gave me to the waves of Ganga, there was still one piece of her writing that I had retained as a mark of my earthly attachment. I re-read the lines: 'These fourteen days with you have left little more to desire of life. I would fulfil my *karma* if, in the next birth, we could spend three days on the banks of Ganga in Benares.

May you be loved to the point of madness. Your mad love Jaya.'

But she was in Karachi. How had she reached Delhi? Was the telegram from Karachi or from Delhi? Was it really she who had sent the telegram? Was she divorcing? Had she abandoned the gods who had described the sacred 'seven-circles' around her marriage? Was she betraying fire, her promise of fidelity? Dream? Hallucination?

Without disturbing anyone in the house, I prepared to leave for Ganga. I woke Ram Lal.

'Jee sahib, jee sahib,' he got up in a huff.

'Sorry to wake...'

'Your orders, *sahib?*'

'Awfully sorry, Ram Lal. Please ask Sanjay to meet me at the Hanuman temple at seven. Don't worry, there was nothing worrying in the telegram.'

'Where are you going, *sahib?*'

'To the *ghats*.'

'I beg your pardon, *sahib*, but it's not very safe at night. The banks of Gangaji at the fort are infested with criminals. No, *sahib*, there are...'

'Please, Ram Lal. I know what I'm doing, See you there with Sanjay.'

I must have walked for about fifteen minutes before I hit the ramparts of the sixteenth century fort constructed by Emperor Akbar. On the dusty path leading to the main entry, beggars and lepers, wrapped in rags and plastic covers, were freezing in the chill of an Allahabadian winter.

I went past them a bit guiltily and found myself a quiet corner behind the fort.

On my left, Ganga lay lazily, an enormous python still asleep, least affected by the agony on her banks — Gods alone can lie back and sleep while the earth lives the tortures of its unions and disunions. I was gripped by a strange sentiment. It was neither pain, nor sorrow, nor nostalgia. Words, images, thoughts, nothing captured it. Just sensations, like waves playing on golden sand, flowed within my body. Call it happiness, call it beatitude, call it the Benares of Jaya's arrivals, all I knew was that something intense and clitoral was embracing me within. Come, my pilgrim, said Ganga, I shall lend you the eye to unravel the invisible. Deep within me, I saw Jaya packing her bags for a journey into the unknown.

The magic of Ganga had enveloped me completely when someone tapped me on the shoulder, and a squeaky voice pierced my ears:

'*Pind daan*, you want to make *pind daan?*'

'No,' I answered firmly.

'If you wish, I could arrange for the *pind daan*,' said the man, with a suspicious smile.

'No, I want nothing.' I thought I was about to be mugged.

'You've asked someone else for the *pind daan*, have you?'

'But what on earth is *pind daan?*'

'Funny! You've come to immerse the ashes in Gangaji, and you don't even know that you have to make a *pind daan!*'

'But, *bhaiya*, what is *pind daan?* I've never heard of it.'

'Offering. It's an offering of food.'

'What food?'

'Auspicious food. It's food for the heavens. Strange, you don't know what *pind daan* is! It's an offering of food for those in heaven.'

'Which heaven?'

'O *baba!* It seems I'll have to explain it all. *Pind daan* is an offering of seventeen *jowahar* flour balls in the memory of the dead. Come, *sahib*, I'll arrange for your offering.'

'But I've lost no-one in the family.'

'Then whose ashes have you come to immerse?'
'Nobody's. Who told you I was here to immerse ashes?'
'Thank the gracious Gangaji that no-one has died in your family! But, you see, that's why there are seventeen balls. It's for the seventeen closest relatives. One for your grandfather, one for your grandmother, grand-uncle, grand-aunt... You see, for seventeen relatives... *Pind daan* is food for anyone of them. It's always good to make this offering, for your grandfather, great grandfather, his ancestors, anyone who has left the earth. With this *daan*, their spirits will be well-nourished and remain in peace...'

'Sorry *bhaiya*, I've lost no-one in the family. I've...'

'You mean not even one of the seventeen has died?' The man was literally wishing that someone around me die, so he could make a buck from his *pind daan*.

'No.'

'But I don't just do *pind daans*. I can arrange for ceremonies for the welfare of your family, for their prosperity, for their health.'

I started walking away very tactfully towards the open, for the threat of a physical assault had not altogether disappeared. He followed at a safe distance behind me, trying perhaps to reassure me that his intention was nothing but religious service. When I had reached a lamp-post, I turned around and reasserted:

'Excuse me, *bhaiya* I haven't come for any religious work. I have no ceremonies to perform!'

'But there's nothing religious about making an offering of food to your ancestors. It's food, just like what we eat every day. But, tell me, *sahib*, can I be of any other help to you?'

'Yes. Just leave me alone.'

'Alone? Who's not alone on this earth? Everyone is alone. And for women, we do special fertility ceremonies. Do you have children, *sahib?*'

'For God sake, can't you leave me to my peace?'

Without budging an inch from where he stood, he fell silent for a few seconds and then, following me stealthily again, he asked:

'Are you a film actor, *sahib*? Are you here for Amitabh Bachchan's election campaign?'

'No,' I snapped.

'You must be a tourist, then!'

'Yes, I am. Any objections?'

'Don't get angry, *sahib*. I can find you a hotel. It's better than spending nights on Gangaji. It's dangerous.'

'Please leave me alone.' I folded my hands and requested him to leave.

'I have hotels of all classes and rates, *sahib*. Cheap hotels like the English country-inns. Five-star hotels like those in America. I am at your service, *sahib*.' He took out a bunch of visiting cards and attempted to hand me one.

'But I don't want a hotel.'

'What service could I then perform for you, *sahib*. After all, you are our guest in Allahabad.'

'Nothing. Just leave me alone.'

'But it's my duty to help you, sir. Medicine, herbs, horoscopes, fortune-telling, I can offer anything you need. We've been asked by the gods to help pilgrims.'

'I'm not a pilgrim,' I roared in anger.

'Strange!' He remarked, with a tinge of sarcasm, 'You're not a pilgrim! You're not a tourist! Nobody has ever died in your family! May I ask you what you're doing here?'

The best way to get rid of the obnoxious rogue was probably to tell him the truth. I said:

'I am a traveller. I'm going down Ganga in a boat. From Gaumukh to Gangasagar.'

'And from Allahabad to?'

'From Allahabad to Benares.'

'Oh! Maybe I can find you a boat, then?'

'No, thank you. I have one.' Turning towards the *ghat* where our boat was anchored, I said: 'You see that boat there. The red one.'

'But that's an official boat!'

'Yes, I'm going in an official boat.'

'Oh! Oh! I'm sorry, *sahib*.' Suddenly, the man looked worried and alarmed. 'Forgive me if I've done anything wrong, *sahib*.'

'No, no. Don't worry. I'm not an officer. Just an ordinary traveller going down Ganga.'

'Ah! Yes, *sahib*. Maybe, then, you'd like this pamphlet on the life of Ganga*ji*.'

The Ganga pamphlet was indeed a rare insight into the contemporary life of an age-old myth. The cover picture of Goddess Ganga was little different from the hottest sex-symbol of the Bombay cinema. Undressed to her flashy panties and bra, stretched backwards in an erotic arch, Ganga seemed more to have arrived from the sets of commercial cinema than from the kingdom of the heavens. The ingenious sketcher of the pamphlet-Ganga, who could well have been a make-up artist from Bombay, had taken every care to lend the Goddess every trait of contemporaneity: rouge, mascara, nail-polish, lipstick. Had he a bit more imagination or with some travel to his credit, he would probably have shown Ganga descend from the heavens with a vanity case in one hand and the latest number of *Vogue* in the other...

Sanjay arrived at seven at the Fort *ghat* and we walked down to the boat. Painted in thick red and white stripes, equipped with two luxury cushions, the motor-boat of the flood-control department looked like a science-fiction spaceship compared to the leaking and rusty skim-boats I had been accustomed to.

Jagdish and Om Prakash, the new crew of boatmen, were *mallahs*, traditional boatmen whose ancestors had helped the gods cross the turbulent river. The only change in the inventory of goods on board was the six jerry-cans of petrol needed for the motor. Om Prakash was all set to announce yet another day on Ganga when the agent, the Gangetic pimp I had met earlier on, arrived panting, and requested:

'Would you accord me a minute, *sahib*?'

'What have you come to sell now, my friend?'

'No, *sahib*. No, *sahib*. Please, please, sir, can I have a minute with you in private?' He sounded hesitant, quite unlike himself.

'Yes, sure.'

'This gentleman, *sahib*,' he said, pointing to a man who stood by an enormous box, 'he's my uncle.'

'And what about him?'

'He has lost someone in his family.'

'I'm sorry to hear that.'

'But you can help him sir.' Was he going to ask me to perform *pind daan* for his uncle?

'How?'

'He has to reach a village near Vindhyachal. The village is on the banks of Gangaji.' If he went by bus, it would take him a good part of the day. He will miss the cremation. I shall be eternally grateful if you could give him a ride.'

'Sure, ask him to hop on.' Stout, arrogant-looking, dressed all in white, the uncle posed no problems, but his enormous rusted steel-trunk certainly did. The gentleman had barely entered the boat when he tripped on something and knocked the petrol jerry-cans off their precarious balance. Sanjay and the boatmen raised their eyebrows disapprovingly, but I quickly whispered: 'He has lost someone in his family.'

The boatmen did their habitual *puja*, and we were off. At

Sangam, the divine union of Ganga, Jamuna and the invisible Saraswati, the three rivers, Om Prakash tilted the rudder sharply and the boat started to rapidly spin on its axis. As if in a whirlpool, the head turned dizzy, the eyes defocused disturbingly, the murky Ganga revolved around Jamuna, and Jamuna around Ganga. One, two, three, four... seven auspicious circles and the boat cruised ahead to the east, towards the rising sun, towards Kashi, towards Benares, towards the holy city where even the 'jingle of pebbles produces music...' That Jaya should have chosen this city as the place of our rebirth was indeed the greatest fortune that I could desire in a world where desire itself was a trapping. May Kashi be Jaya and Jaya, Kashi. As Jaya said so often: 'May all brides be Benares born...'

Ganga by now had become a trustworthy friend. Her surprises had become familiar and her moods, predictable. Though the draught in the river was good, Jagdish sat in front for navigation and Ram took the tail. Seeing an abandoned jute-cot on the right bank, Om Prakash explained that in Hinduism all the belongings of the dead were floated on Ganga with the dead body. 'It's even holier,' remarked Jagdish, 'to float the dead just before they have actually died. To entrust an almost-dead to Ganga is much holier than an already-dead.' For a good half-hour, the boat serpented past multiple dead bodies floating on the river. To reincarnate nightmares not yet forgotten, some bodies offered themselves to the devouring appetite of dogs, and when we passed the immensely bloated dead body of a dog, Sanjay exclaimed: 'This bastard must have died of over-eating corpses!'

From dawn to dusk, Ganga offers a varied spectacle. The first to wake on her banks is the gentle glow of dawn. The birds arrive next. Then the cacophony is joined by hundreds of men, women and children who come to the banks for their morning ablutions. As the sun rises further, the mornings on Ganga begin to resemble the rush-hours of the metropoles: busy and nervous movements, cattle bathing, people washing, women dressing... Past the early hours when the men folk have disappeared into the fields, it is the women, with a child on one hip and a brass pot on the head, who keep Ganga company through the piercing cries of their children. When the day turns bright yellow, the river is entrusted to those for whom she is the only source of livelihood. Labourers, fishermen, boatmen, it is they who escort Ganga through her hottest hours and it is again they who offer the sacred waters a whiff of their sweat and toil.

As we made our way towards Benares, the boat attracted every living glance on the shores. Excited children, puzzled women, intrigued men and even spellbound animals, struck by the unusual sound of a motor-boat, looked wonderingly at the purring machine. Hundreds of young boys and girls rushed to the bank, yelling, screaming, jeering, cheering, and how could I forget the boy riding a buffalo who, eager to catch a sight of the boat, lunged forward and fell flat into the river with his animal. Looking at this spectacle, it seemed that the banks of Ganga had hardly changed since the beginning of the last century: 'When steamers first appeared in India, inhabitants flocked in thousands to the river to worship them and implore mercy, believing them to be the engines of supernatural creation.'

Around mid-day, the sun was beginning to get hot when Sanjay stretched towards his food basket and pulled out a bottle wrapped in a wet towel. Breaking the seal he said: 'Let's have some fun. Long time since one felt light.'

'It won't look nice.'

'What do you mean?'

'This chap won't appreciate it.' I remarked, pointing towards the gentleman on his way to a cremation.

'Balls! We haven't lost anyone, have we?' Sanjay said in a

flat, matter-of-fact tone. 'At this rate, we'll never get to have a drink. Don't be such a humanist, my friend. Humanism makes you weak.'

'Come, come. It doesn't look nice. And then, he should be getting off any moment now.' I persisted.

'Balls! Let's have some fun, ole chap, before diabetes and heart attacks catch up with us.' Sanjay poured the gin into two glasses. Watching us, Om Prakash smiled mischievously.

'*Arre*, Om, will you have some?' I asked, showing him the bottle.

'No, thanks, *sahib*, I don't drink.'

'Come, come, don't be shy. Have some.'

'I don't drink, *sahib*.'

'Nothing?'

'No intoxication *sahib*.'

'Liar,' I said, jokingly.

'Some *ganja* at times, sir. Never any drinks. No-one has ever had alcohol in my family, *sahib*.'

'It's a sin, is it?'

'No *sahib*. It makes you lose control of yourself.'

'Come, come. *Ganja* is no better.'

'But alcohol is worse *sahib*. There was a Mahatma once who received a woman. She was carrying some meat and alcohol on her. Over the course of her meeting with the Mahatma, she fell in love with him and wanted the Mahatma to give her his body. The Mahatma was in a big fix. When Mahatma refused, the woman asked him to choose between three things—meat, alcohol, her body. If he didn't accept, the woman threatened to defame him. The Mahatma, being a high caste Brahmin, could not accept to eat meat nor could he afford to make love. So he chose alcohol. Having got drunk, he succumbed to the rest. Ate meat, made love. No *sahib*, I'm afraid of alcohol.'

'Yes, you're right.' commented the agent's uncle, 'but *ganja* is worse. I can tell you so many stories about the harm that *ganja* can do. I think what matters is the proportion. In small doses, everything is fine.'

'Ask him if he wants some.' Sanjay suggested.

'Are you mad? He's lost someone in his family!'

'He doesn't look too disturbed, does he? He's been fooling around with the boatmen all along.'

'You ask. I can't.'

Ganga was turning blurry by the second round of drinks when the gentleman-mourner on board leaned towards me and asked with a nosy curiosity:

'What's that you're drinking?'

'Gin.'

'Gin? What's that?'

'English wine.'

'Oh! What does it taste like?'

'Light and nice. One feels a bit high.'

'Could I try some? Just a drop.'

'Yes, sure. I'm sorry we didn't offer you any before. We didn't dare...'

'Why? I'm sufficiently grown-up to handle such small intoxications in life.'

'We thought you might not like a drink under the sad circumstances.'

'Sad circumstances? What's happened?'

'You've lost someone in your family, haven't you?'

'I? Lost someone in my family? *Hare, hare, hare...* God forbid! Whoever told you that?'

'The man who introduced you to me said that you had to reach Vindhyachal today for a cremation. He said you had lost someone in your family.'

'That agent? That bastard! These agents would do anything for money. Scoundrels! He told me that there was a boat going to Vindhyachal and if I wished I could go on the boat for fifty rupees. He took fifty rupees for the fare and fifteen rupees as his commission. Oh God! What a rascal! If I ever see him again, I'll wring his neck.' He was livid with anger. I felt no better at having been taken for an easy prey. The uncle asked:

'But tell me, that swine, did he give you any money?'

'No, nothing.'

'*Hare Gange, Hare Gange.* What a swine! He didn't give you the fifty rupee note?'

'No.'

'I'll beat him to pulp on my return. He's walked off with sixty-five rupees. And now I'll have to pay you on top of that.'

'Don't worry about us. We're not a transport company.'

'So kind of you. So kind of you, indeed. Thank Ganga, that there are still bountiful souls left on this earth. Otherwise the world is full of scoundrels.'

He downed the gin in one shot like a pub regular and let out a long sigh, the sorrow of having lost a fifty rupee note. Pouring himself another drink, which was twice the size of the first, he remarked thoughtfully:

'Something should be done about these crooks. I'm going to take it up with our association.'

'What do you do in Allahabad?' asked Sanjay.

'Public service.'

'In the government, are you?'

'No, no. Religious services for the common man.'

'What sort?'

'I am a *panda*.' Sanjay and I exchanged a quick glance, knowing that the *pandas*, the ancient mediators between the living and the heavens, had by now become the pimps of the religious underworld.

'Ah! *Panda!*' exclaimed Sanjay, 'I've heard so much about them, but never really got round to finding out much about this profession. Who exactly is a *panda*?'

'Strange! Are you a Hindu?'

'Yes.'

'You're a Hindu, and you don't know who a *panda* is! When someone dies, we perform the ceremony for the immersion of ashes in Ganga. Again, when you wish to make a *daan*, it is the *pandas* who do it for you. At one time it was considered one of the noblest professions on earth. Well, not really a profession, a pious service for humanity.'

'At one time! Why, isn't it a noble profession today!'

'Of course, it still remains the duty of honest and learned people. But you know all sorts of people have entered the profession. For instance, in Allahabad alone, there are thousands of *pandas*. Not all are honest. But I'm a *khandani panda*. They call me *Kali Kamli wale Punjabi purohit*. I'm the established *panda* for everyone from Punjab.'

'Do you mean to say,' quipped Sanjay sarcastically, 'that among *pandas* too, you have a state cadre? If I'm looking for a *panda* to perform some ceremony, do I go by scholarship or by regional designation?'

'Scholarship, certainly, yes. But, first, by the man in charge of that region. Anyone from Punjab, for instance, must come to me.'

'Must? Why? Are you appointed by the government?'

'No, no. By Gangaji's blessings, this is one area where the government still hasn't messed up things. We're Punjab *pandas* by tradition.'

'You mean someone from Punjab can't go to anyone else.'

'By all means, he can. But what's the point when his records are with me.'

'What records?'

'Oho! You really have no idea about our profession. You see, we have a record register which has the names and addresses of all the people who have had religious services performed. To give you an example, where are you from?' the *panda* asked me.

'From Rajasthan.'

'Pity. I don't have your records.'

'But I'm from Punjab.' said Sanjay.

'Splendid!' exclaimed the *panda*, 'Now, do you remember the name of anyone in your family whose ashes were brought to Ganga?'

'Yes, my grandfather's.

'His name?'

'Baldev Singh.

'From which district?'

'Amritsar.'

'Which *tehsil*?

'Ajnala.'

'Now wait a minute. All I want is patience. Don't you worry, I'll dig out the reference.'

Belching out gin bubbles, the *panda* got up from his seat and staggered towards his steel trunk. Om Prakash left the rudder and helped him open the box. The *panda* pulled out an enormous register, the thickest I had ever seen in my life. Red in colour, the register which resembled the 'record book of the heavens', was a perfect square, one metre in length and width, and at least half-a-metre in thickness. It was beautifully manuscripted, and if the *panda* was to be believed, its market price was more than that of a decent mansion in Allahabad.

'Now, what did you say the *tehsil* was?'

'Ajnala,' reminded Sanjay.

The *panda* found the relevant section and started reading out names with a constant drone which, strangely, resembled that of the motor boat: 'ram singh son of harnam singh mukha singh son of pritam singh harmeek singh son of mukhtiar singh pyara singh son of harbeer singh zara singh jarnail singh son of laftain singh muhabbat singh son of nikamma singh pratap singh son of hari singh ramrakha sing son of mun shiramharpartal singh son of joginder singh harmeet singh son of avtar singh rameshwar singh son of jugadha singh joginder singh son of hushiar singh mudhala singh son of jatala singh dhillon bhagwan singh son of mudhalar singh shakti singh son ofhari singh milki singh son of ramkripasi jagdish singh son of ramrakhatwat singh harnam singh son of rajpal singh mann partap singh kairon son of surjit singh kairon gurdial singh son of......'

'What did you say the name was?'

'Baldev Singh. But listen *panditji*...'

'Hang on, hang on, hang on,' Panda raised him arm to demand patience. 'we'll find it here. You're sure his ashes came here?'

'Yes, yes, I'm positive.'

'I'm sure we'll find it.'

'But listen, *panditji*, we can...'

'Hang on now, don't disturb.' The *panda* started off again:

'karnail singh son of captaan singh harjatta singh son of bachittar singh pyareram son of khushiram lalluram son of karyadapadduram son of laladh singh karem singh dev singh kuldip singh son of durgadevi mehtaab singh son of faryan singh prakash singh son of hawaldar singh hawaldar singh son of jarnail singh mukaddar singh kerainwale son of faujasmgh...'

'*Panditji Panditji*' We intervened to halt the agonizing flood of names, 'Listen...'

'Stop it, please! This is normal, such things take time. At times it takes three days to find the right page... Sardar singh son of hakeem singh avatram son of karnail singh vijakat son of fakeer singh baldev singh... Ah! Here it is–Baldev Singh' Now what was his father's name?'

'Sardar Singh.'

'Correct. It's marked here. See.' The *panda* tilted the book slightly towards us. With a triumphant laugh, he announced to everyone in the boat: 'There you are! There you are! You want to know other details about your grandfather? He had one hundred *bighas* of land, his wife's name was Isri Devi. He had six children, four sons and three daughters.'

'How many children?' asked Sanjay, as if cross-checking.

'Six children. Four sons and three daughters.'

'But *panditji*, how can this be? Six children, with four sons and three daughters. Something wrong somewhere, isn't it?' Sanjay said, laughing.

'Small errors could be possible but, otherwise, this record register is more accurate than our national census. It goes back to the days of the first Sikh Guru, way back to the fifteenth century. Now you see why people from Punjab come to me. If you like, *sahib*, I could do a *pind daan* for your grandfather right here and now.'

'No thanks. Another time, but tell me...'

'Seriously, *pind daan* is a very holy ritual. You wouldn't like to send some food to your ancestors?'

'Another time, *panditji*. At the moment I don't have enough for myself! But tell me, can no other *panda* accept a person from Punjab?'

'By all means he can. But people prefer to come to the one who has their family records. That's why I said that a record book is more valuable than a mansion in Allahabad.'

The *panda*, having won the first battle of honour, went back and sat on his seat. Feeling lighter and lighter under the effect of the 'English wine', he asked for another drink.

'Is this your only profession?' I asked, noticing that the holy *panda* sounded quite a wheeler-dealer.

'Let's say this is my main profession. I live off this and donations.'

'That must be an awfully small income then?'

'Depends. Some *pandas* are quite well off. At times they make up to 100,000 rupees with one single client!'

'Gosh! That's the top income-tax slab!'

'No. No. Thank Ganga there's no tax on religious donations!'

'How much do you make, *panditji*? I asked cheekily.

'I'm a small man but god has been kind to me. Some pandas make a thousand rupees a day. And during the January *mela*, they make a fortune. They are very rich–buildings, trucks, travel agencies, they own all sorts of things. They're big enough to influence politicians and senior officers of the state administration.'

'I guess it's a question of being known in the region one's looking after, isn't it?'

'Not entirely. Clients are brought by agents who take fifty per cent of the *daan*.'

'Do you have agents?'

'No, not me, I love being alone. I don't exploit people's sentiments. Then my business is well-established. Ganga*ji* has been kind. One of my sons is a lawyer.'

'Lawyer? He didn't follow in your footsteps?'

'Yes, yes, he's very much with me. During the day, he is at the courts and early mornings he comes to my office on the *ghats*. But, you see, things are getting worse day by day. The basic source of wealth is records. Now, as the family grows, the records register can't be divided. It's the region from where the pilgrims come which is subdivided among sons. So the source of wealth gets smaller and smaller with each new child.'

'That's like land,' observed Sanjay.

'Slightly different. Land gets reduced with population but, in our business, population increase can also mean more clients and pilgrims.'

'How wonderful! Sanjay exclaimed aloud, bursting into laughter, 'Marvellous! Yours is the only profession in the world which gains as much from birth-rate as from the rate of mortality. Bravo!'

'But Gangaji is great and her bounty limitless.' The *panda* leaned over the boat and, his hands forming a cup, he scooped out some holy water. Drinking with a long slurp, he chanted: '*Haregange, Haregange, Haregange,* you're the mother of all universe. Long live Ganga, you're the source of prosperity, wealth and health.'

With his gin-shot eyes and drowsy movements, the *panda* had not quite dozed off for a nap when the boat, making its way through a channel close to the bank, was attacked by some young urchins. Hurling insults, calling us names, the boys attacked the boat with stones and slush-balls. Om raced to pull the boat out of the line of attack, and Sanjay and I ducked, covering our heads with cushions. Everyone escaped unhurt except the poor *panda* who, a shade sluggish in his reflexes, thanks to his love of English wine, got a stone right on his chest. 'Bastards! Bastards!' he shouted, 'Criminals! Gangaji is full of criminals! I don't know why our wretched administration can't do anything about these hooligans!'

Sanjay, the symbol of the state on board, looked into the *panda's* eyes, and said sarcastically: '*Panditji*, it's not easy to fight crime. It's as difficult to fight these hooligans on the banks as the *pandas* on the *ghats* of Ganga...' The *panda* was to discover soon that the gentleman from Punjab he had been talking to was, in fact, a senior official in the Allahabad administration.

Having learnt that, the *panda* flattered and fawned over Sanjay. And just before leaving the boat, he implored:

'*Sahib*, I have a little favour to ask of you. I have this disputed property in Allahabad which...'

Bhajan-Benares

Bhola mana jane
Amar meri kaya

Dhan re joban
Sapne si maya
Badal ki si chaya

Aik kuan paanch panihari
Jal bharti hain nyari

Dat jayega kouan
Sookh jayegi kyari
Hath mal mal chali
Panchon panihari

Sookha sa kaath
Det nahin Chaya
Kahan tera hansa
kahan teri maya

Baloo ki bheet
Pavan ka khamba
Deval dekh
Bhaya achambha

Aadi aadinath
Manchdar ka poota

Gaye jas jo mera
Gorakh avadhoota...

Om, as his name evoked, had deep mystery in his voice. Devotional, mystical, sensual, erotic, whatever the genre, he mastered them all. Holding the oar flat in his hand, Om sang long, and the more he sang the more he looked transported into another universe. With each couplet over, he opened his eyes, became earthy and blushed, as if hypnotized by the beauty of his own voice. A magician given oars in his hands to earn a livelihood, Om took one single phrase of the devotional song, the same words, the same syllables, and played with them in his breath until the words secreted a rainbow. With slight inflexions, Om's voice, a kaleidoscope of sounds and words, detached meaning from word, and sound from meaning: *mana*, the soul, sung in deep resonance, invoked the mystical self, and *mana*, the same soul made to slide along the slopes of breath, invoked the urgent sensuality in mind, the urge to exchange a glance with the Goddess right here and now. Om demonstrated with such effortless ease that the word written had one meaning and the word sung so many. Word, sound and meaning are infinite, said Om, as the waters of Ganga whose origins and ends no-one shall ever know.

'He sang the *bhajan* for you, *bhaiya*.' Jagdish whispered to me.
'Why for me?' I was surprised.
'That was Om's gift for the auspicious day.'
'You mean to Ganga?'
'No, to you.'
'What auspicious day?'
'Because didn't you tell us that Jaya *behan* was arriving in Benares today?'
'Oh! How thoughtful of you, Om. I am touched. You sing

so well. Did you ever learn to sing?'

'No, *bhaiya*. I haven't been to any *gurus*. For the boatmen, song comes to them from an inner need. My whole life has been spent on Gangaji. When I was four, my father gave me an oar in my hand. Ever since, Ganga has been my life. A boatman consoles himself with a song.'

'I've heard other boatmen sing too, but your voice has a deep classical quality. I thought you'd trained it, Om.'

'So kind of you, *bhaiya*, but I sing for fun. Without music, it's difficult to live through this long and painful life.'

'You sound sad, Om.'

'Life is sad.'

'Come, come, what makes you so gloomy on this beautiful morning?' Om looked away. Lighting a *beedi*, he picked up the oar and started rowing again. After a long silence, he turned towards me and said musingly:

'Arrivals are beautiful.'

'Yes, they can be. But you sound sad, Om?'

'No, *sahib*. I was just thinking about something. Did you say that Jaya *behan* was twenty-five?'

'Yes.'

'My wife was also twenty-five.'

'Was?'

'She died last year. The last I went to Benares was to see her.'

'What happened?'

'Dysentery.'

'Couldn't the doctors treat that? Dysentery is nothing!'

'Long story, *bhaiya*. The truth is that she died, and died young. It all happened in two days. One night in Allahabad, I got a telegram asking me to reach Benares. I reached and she was already on her death-bed.'

'Tragic!'

'People come into our lives, they leave. The wheel of life keeps turning. Strange!' After a brief thoughtful silence, Om asked:

'Don't you think, *bhaiya*, all that remains of a relationship is its beginning and its end? The rest is unimportant. All I remember of my wife is our marriage and her cremation-pyre... Strange, and yet life goes on....' Turning his glance away, Om plunged the oars violently into the river and began to hum a Mira *bhajan* which evoked her meeting with Lord Krishna.

It all began in Paris. It was early October. Leaves were turning yellow and brown, and there was a palish beauty about the streets of Paris. A gentle autumn drizzle glistened on Rue Hallé. There was something pre-natal about the night. I don't know why I felt a sudden desire to go back to the umbilical cord and I decided to pay homage to the man, the only man, whose memory had made me quit the ravaged factories of the Indian Far Left, and travel to Paris.

Late at night, or was it early morning, I walked across the whole city. Denfert-Rochereau, Raspail, Hôtel de Lassay, Louvre, Opera, Place de Clichy; I walked to the Cimetière de Batignolles. The cemetery was shut. That, in the west, even the dead needed padlocks on their graves amused me, but I took the side-lane and jumped over the wall. Raindrops tapped gently on chestnut leaves, the dead smelt fresh. Following Elisa's instructions, I went down the dark tunnel of *tilleul* trees and turned right, when, strangely, the smell of sweat hit me in the face. I stopped, looked around; there was no-one. I turned left again on the Thirty-First Avenue of the cemetery. It was pitch dark. I looked left and saw a little oil-lamp go off, as if somebody had switched off the lights on my arrival. Curious, I walked up to the grave and lit the lamp. In the flickering flame, I read the most famous literary epitaph of the last century inscribed in black: '*Je cherche l'or du temps, André Breton 1896-1966.*' I re-read the lines, and knew that the man who had indefatigably 'searched the gold of times' had never died... The mystery of the oil lamp was beginning to intrigue me when I noticed, on the lowest step of the grave, distinct traces of an Indian offering: coconut, sacred thread, jaggery, marigold petals, and another lamp with a burnt wick in the middle of an old silver plate. On a white sheet of paper, wet and soiled, there were the smudged remains of a poem. The only line I could read was: 'this night of molten silver, this breath of autumnal desires...'

Some ten graves away, with her back turned towards me, a girl sat smoking a cigarette. Hearing my footsteps, she struck a match, rendering her presence bewitchingly naked. Dark complexioned, long black hair, wearing white pyjamas and a bright yellow silken *kurta*... She smiled, a smile that comes to so few so naturally. She lit another match, and looked up towards me from that precise angle where a woman's eye can make its most lethal assault. I saw a flock of birds flap out of her hair, as rain trickled down her slender neck. Then, again, she looked away, her eyes describing that perfect arch of a beach along which Ganga would love to sleep forever.

'Was that you?' I murmured, holding my breath.

'What?'

'That silver platter?'

'Yes.'

'You jumped over the wall too?' The wall was rather high I had noticed.

'No. I just stayed on after sunset. Nobody asked me to leave.'

'What brings you here?'

'*Je cherche l'or du temps!*' She reveried, lighting another cigarette.

'What brings you here? Love or theft?'

'Theft,' she chortled. 'The jewels of Nadja!'

'Ah! You know Nadja!' I was a bit surprised.
'Who doesn't?'
'Do you believe in spirits?'
'Who doesn't?'
'Do you think it's Nadja's spirit who's doing this tonight?'
'Doing what?'
'This. Our meeting.'
'Possible. Or he?' She said, pointing towards André Breton's grave.
'You mean André?'
'Yes.'
'No. He was because Nadja was.'
'And Nadja was because he was!'
'Rubbish! He was because Nadja was.'
'But who was Nadja?' She asked with genuine curiosity.
'She was a woman.'
'Any woman?'
'No. A woman who went mad.'
'She didn't go mad. People thought she went mad. So you too think she went mad?'
'She was a woman who was as real as unreal.'
'I am too, as real as unreal.' She got up briskly, turned towards me and, looking straight in my eyes, declared: 'I am Nadja.'
'Then I am André!' I answered, with a nervous laugh.
'You know you're not André but I know I am Nadja. After her death, she was reborn a Hindu. That's me–Jaya!. Did you know Nadja's body?'
'Yes.'
'Could you identity it?'
'She had a crescent mark on her breast.'
'This one!' She unbuttoned her *kurta*, and burst out laughing. 'So now you believe me! Do you know where Nadja died?'

'In an asylum in Paris.'

'Wrong! In Shanghai. As they say, under mysterious circumstances.' Then she whispered to herself: 'I shouldn't be saying this.'

'Why.'

'Because I promised.'

'What?'

'That I'd never disclose who I was.'

'And now?'

'I've broken my promise on his grave.'

'Do you think he can see you?'

'Perhaps. He could see everything. Come, let's get away.'

We walked out of the cemetery.

'Look!' said Jaya, pointing to the rear of a van. 'See what it says?' An advertisement on it said: 'Eat honey, live better.' Jaya laughed and, looking up at the sky with abandon, she murmured: 'Eat stars, live better!' We walked down the boulevard up to the main square when Jaya said:

'My foot's hurting. Let's take a taxi.'

'But I love walking.'

'And I love speed!' Just then, a taxi stopped right by us. Jaya opened the door. The taxi driver asked her:

'Where are you going, Mademoiselle?'

'Wherever you are going, Monsieur!' Jaya answered with a soliciting smile. Excited, the driver switched off the taxi and whispered to Jaya:

'Come, I'll take you to the moon!'

'You're crazy. I've just returned from there.'

'OK, I'll take you wherever you want to go.'

'I want you to drive at 200 kilometres per hour, against the flow of traffic, right into a one-way street. Do you agree?'

'She's drunk!' The driver started the taxi and drove off.

I can only recall fragments of that night. Cobble-stones. Drizzle. Little traffic on the roads. A torn poster of *Rue Case Negre*. *Le Pen* posters on the walls. A *clochard* on a bicycle. La Seine. Triangular street lamps. Jaya tapped me on my shoulder and asked:

'Do you know who got these lamps installed?'

'I think it was during Napoleon III's epoch.'

'But who?'

'Someone in his administration.'

'No. It was me.'

'You? How?'

'Before being born as Nadja, I was Marie-Christine de Bucci, one of the Emperor's mistresses. One night, Napoleon asked me to decorate the nights of Paris. I had the triangular street lamps installed. So you see you're learning a bit about the history of this city!'

'During Napoleon's epoch, there was a man...'

'Let me ask you something,' interrupted Jaya, with an air of urgency, 'tell me what happened after I died?'

'You mean after the mistress died?'

'No, after Nadja died.'

'In the first year, nothing much happened. Then, André Breton published his famous prose-poem.'

'What prose-poem?'

'The famous book, *Nadja*.'

'Cheat! What a rascal!'

'Why?'

'He promised me he wouldn't write about me.'

'Well, he did.'

'And then?'

'Within weeks, *Nadja* became the legend of modern French literature. The book was all over the place. It even reached the mental asylums. The inmates devoured it. The jailers campaigned to have the book banned!'

'Did André get to find out that I had fled the asylum?'

'No.'

'He didn't know that I went to Shanghai?'

'Not that I can recall. And you know what, scores of girls used to call his wife after his death. They all claimed they were Nadja...'

'Look!' Jaya pointed towards a cafe.

'What about it?'

'You see that cafe–*La Nuit des hasards!* That's where André and I had our last drink.'

'Shall we step in there to have our first?'

Jaya suddenly stopped, tugging at my coat pocket. Her face tautened, her eye-balls shifted rapidly, as if she were contemplating a conspiracy. A heavy silence and then, saying 'Fine' to herself, she took off her sapphire ring from the left hand and slipped it on the index finger of the other hand. Laughing nervously, she said:

'Do you follow that?'

'Your ring changed hands.'

'Why?'

'You tell me.'

'That's my other life. Jaya's life. Promise me you won't speak a word about Nadja and André Breton at the cafe. Not a word.'

'I promise. But why?'

'Don't ask.'

We stepped into the cafe, where an Arab bartender, exceptionally gregarious for this late hour of night, greeted us:

"Welcome, welcome my friends. I know, I know you're from India! You know Lata Mangeshkar and Raj Kapoor? Oh we love your cinema in Algeria. Dance, music, beautiful women, what a great country! Sit, sit, please sit, my beautiful lady. Pardon me my indulgence, mademoiselle, but if ever a woman like you took a fancy to me, I wouldn't wait a minute before marrying her. Sit, please take a seat...' And even before we had taken off our coats, the bartender had blaring music playing on his system: *'Awaara hoon...'* Jaya, slightly irritated with the barman, ordered two vodkas to buy some peace.

'What does a *diya* mean to you?' I asked Jaya.

'Jyoti, inner light. And to you?'

'The desire to light.'

'And for me, the desire to be lit...'

'Are you a believer?'

'A believer in pagan gods.'

'And your favourite god?'

'Shiva.'

'Shiva, you call him pagan?

'Yes. His dance is pagan.'

'You dance, do you?'

'Yes.'

'What?'

'Mohiniaatam.' Overhearing our conversation, the barman swooped down on our table and exclaimed: 'You dance! I love the Indian dance! Beautiful women, dancing girls, what else do you want in life! Come, come, gulp down your vodkas. I'll get you another two. It's on me.'

As he went to fetch us a second round of drinks, Jaya asked: 'And your favourite god?'

'None.

'Atheist? Gosh, this is becoming like a game! What's your favourite colour?'

'Red.'

'Good heavens!' she said, sending out rings of laughter, 'Red!

Not another Marxist, I hope? Trotskyist?'

'Like him.'

'Like who?'

'Breton.'

'Breton who?'

'André Breton. He wrote the third manifesto of surrealism with Trotsky.'

'Schh! Schh! You've broken your promise...'

Jaya became pensive and distant, as if the name of André Breton had touched in her something deeply fragile. She downed her vodka in one flick, got up and said abruptly: 'Come. Let's leave. Check please!' The barman refused to charge us money. Without thanking him, or smiling back, Jaya, lost in her world of reincarnations, grabbed her coat and walked out. It was still drizzling. We crossed the road. Jaya stopped. She took off the ring from the right hand and slipped it on to the other. The effect was immediate. Jaya became Nadja.

Dawn was about to break over Paris. The bakers were raising their shutters and the early morning traffic was beginning to invade the boulevards. Jaya looked restless, unable to walk straight by my side. When we reached Boulevard St. Martin, she suggested that we play 'crossing roads', a game she had invented.

The game consisted of two partners crossing the street in the midst of traffic, and the one who arrived at the other end first was the winner. 'But this is suicidal, Jaya!' I remarked, looking at cars and buses whizzing down the boulevard. Jaya answered with childish excitement: 'Not at all, it trains our reflexes...' She went first, throwing herself onto a road full of speeding vehicles. Jaya had barely reached the other end when a police patrol-car came to a screeching halt. A *gendarme* got out and walked up towards Jaya.

'What do you think you're doing, Mademoiselle?'

'Crossing roads.'

'Is this the way to cross roads?'

'Which other way is there? In geometry, the easiest crossing is along a straight line between two points. Do you know the Euclidean revolution, Monsieur le Gendarme?' The policeman smirked, unable to decipher her. A second policeman came and joined us.

'May I see your papers, Mademoiselle?' Jaya plunged her hand into her bag and pulled out two booklets–one maroon and the other black.

'Which one would you fancy? Black or maroon?'

'I want your passport, Mademoiselle.'

'They are both mine.'

A deranged person or a terrorist? The cop looked puzzled: 'How do you have two passports?'

'Because I am two persons.'

'What do you mean two persons?'

'Like you are two policemen, in the service of the Fifth French republic. I am two women, both in the service of the surrealist revolution.'

'Which revolution?' asked the cop.

'Surrealist. Do you believe in reincarnation?'

'What?'

'Do you believe in rebirth?'

'She's a nut case.' said one cop to the other. He compared the two passports.

Same photograph, same dates, same visa-stamps. Intrigued, he inquired:

'How do you have two names?'

'Because I am two human beings.' The cops, losing patience with Jaya, asked us to hop in their car and drove off to the Prefecture de Police. 'Paris looks so wonderful from a flying-squad!' whispered Jaya into my ear. I was not sure if it is looked better or worse, Paris certainly looked different. Vehicles on the road vied with each other to make room for the sirening police car. Each time we slowed down at a corner, people rushed out of cafes and bakery-shops and peered curiously into the car. We were on the Conciergerie bridge over the Seine when one of the cops turned back and asked Jaya:

'But how can you be two persons?'

'Simple, by having two passports!' Raising his voice, the policeman asked again:

'But how did you manage to get two different passports, Mademoiselle?'

'By being two different persons, Monsieur... You obviously don't believe me.'

'She's mad.' said one cop to the other.

'Strange!' remarked Jaya, leaning in front, 'do you know, Monsieur, in India, for one god we have 50,000 names. But, yes, they didn't have passports at that time. Though I wonder how the gods travelled from one country to the other.' By now, the cop was busy filling in some grey and brown sheets of paper.

'Your address, Mademoiselle?'

'In India?'

'No, in Paris,' blurted the cop, with authority.

'Last night it was the Cimitière de Batignolles. It changes every night.'

With a lascivious smile on his lips, the cop asked Jaya:

'And your address tonight?'

'Ask the gentleman beside me.'

That's how we met...

'*Bhaiya, bhaiya*,' screamed Om, in excitement, '*bhaiya*, Benares!' Benaras rose gently above the surface of a serene Ganga. Kashi, as Benares was first called, has the most stunning skyline in the world. Slender minarets, round domes, tiered roofs, Saracen arches, rusted tridents, match-stick pillars, sunflower-parasols, windswept *ghats* – this ancient city is an architectural splendour on which the Hindus, the Muslims, the Buddhists and the Jains, all religions save Christianity, have left behind their trace for posterity. History might have known cities where different religions contributed to raise a collective architecture, but it is the sheer simplicity of this fusion in Benares which makes it the sublime solvent of architectural divides. From a distance, the skyline of Benares is even deceptive. Belying the pages of history, Benares, from mid-stream Ganga, looks forgetful, as if it had effaced from its memory the bloody pages of history on which some Afghan, Mughal or Hindu ruler had inscribed the war-cries of plunder and iconoclasm. Jagdish and Ram got up and offered petals to the distant silhouette of the city, then switched off the motor and began rowing towards the Dasaswamedha *ghat*. Looking up towards a sky invaded by cranes and black-breasted *ahingas*, Ram exclaimed: 'Look at the birds, *bhaiya*! Their song is in celebration of her arrival. But, *bhaiya*, don't forget us in the excitement. We won't leave Benares till we've met Jaya *behan*.'

We managed to anchor the boat mid-stream. The Dasaswamedha *ghat* was to our left and the sunrise was to be on the right.

The banks of the river were brimming with pilgrims. Om asked me:

'Do you know why this *ghat* is called Dasaswamedha?'

'Not really. I've read about it somewhere though.'

'*Dasa*, ten, *asawa*, horse, *medha*, sacrifice,' explained Om, 'Dasaswamedha *ghat* means the spot where the ten-horse sacrifice was performed. You see, a long time ago, Lord Shiva was unhappy with the Raja of Kashi because he had been expelling gods and goddesses from his kingdom. So Shiva sent Brahma to Kashi.

The intention was to make the king falter and sin so that, using this pretext, Shiva could then throw him out. Brahma arrived and said to the king that he wanted to perform ten highly complicated horse sacrifices for which he needed twenty-seven different ingredients. The ingredients were very difficult to find. Brahma had suspected that the king would not be able to provide what he had asked for and, therefore, the king could be asked to leave. But the king managed to provide everything. Brahma performed the sacrifices and the Raja was saved.'

'So, for once, Shiva lost to a mortal king.'

'No, no. The story is not over. The king was later persuaded to leave by Shiva's son, Ganesh. Yes, yes, I'm sure the king left but I don't know how… It is common knowledge in Kashi that the king left the city by that narrow street you see behind the *ghat*…'

Om could not remember the rest of the story but, 3000 years after the Raja of Kashi was dethroned, I could see that hundreds of jubilant Japanese tourists had managed to reach the same *ghat* taking the same 'narrow street' by which the king had left. Like swarms of locusts, they arrived with their cameras and knapsacks, as if Brahma had performed all those sacrifices for the pleasures of Japanese tourism. Two short, but robust, Japanese came out of the herd and placed their cameras on tripod stands. One by one, the two semi-professionals started fitting their lenses; one was good enough to pass for an anti-aircraft gun. The tour-guide announced through a portable megaphone: 'Silence! Silence! Ready with your cameras. Sunrise in twenty-five seconds!' The photographers crouched behind their cameras, like hunters all set to shoot down the Hindu-sun…

The sunrise began. First, an orange blotch on the grey sky. Seconds later, the blotch expanded, the sun blowing out an orange glow into space. Then, orange dissolved into pale yellow.

A tiny slice of clementine emerged on the horizon, yellow and aflame. Sensing light in their wings, crows, eagles and vultures began to rise and dive, and the sun looked trapped in a hundred zigzagging barbed wires. Slowly, the sun sliced into two: flame and eclipse, light and darkness. The flame got the better of the eclipse, and, in a flash, it became impossible to look into the sun. Before, we were looking into the sun and now, it looked at us. The sun was born, the world was born, like a yolk pulled out of the egg-shell with a silken thread. Behind us, the tour-guide announced to his troupe: 'Those who could not get the photograph on time can buy picture post-cards at the hotel. Ten rupees for three cards...'

On the *ghats*, Benares wore the costume of Hindu beliefs. As the sun cast on the red-stoned Benares a veil of yellow, making the city blush like a girl, the air was rent with *bhajans* and religious chants. The voice of a *yogi*, belly deep in Ganga, rose above the rest:

> *Ganga cha Yamune chaiva*
> *Godawari Saraswati*
> *Narmade Sindhu Kaveri*
> *Jale asmin sannidhim kuru.*

People bathing, chanting, meditating, performing the *suryapranam*—Ganga received a million greetings for her morn. *Pandas* woke under their palm-leaf umbrellas to another day of money-making. Excited children and belief-struck women offered lamps to the river-goddess. On the top steps of the *ghat*, young men were doing body-building exercises. Seeing the wrestlers exercise, I thought of the medieval European travellers who had mistaken these simple acts of body-building for some obscure act of Hindu belief. Long ago, a French jewel-merchant called Tavernier wrote, after his travel to Benares: 'An example of a strange kind of penance which I saw while sailing up the Ganges on the 12th May 1666. A clean place on the margin of the river had been prepared, in which one of these poor idolaters was condemned to place himself on the ground many times during the day, supported only on his hands and feet, and to kiss the ground three times before rising, without daring to touch it with the rest of his body. When he rose it was necessary for him to do so on the left foot, with the right foot in the air, and every morning during a whole month, before drinking or eating, he was obliged to place himself in this position fifty times in succession, and kiss the ground one hundred and fifty times. I was told that the Brahmins had inflicted this penance on him for having allowed the cow to die in his house, not having taken it to the margin of the water in accordance with the custom, in order that it might be bathed while dying...' Monsieur Tavernier, jewel-merchant-traveller, I respect you for your travelogue, but this 'strange kind of penance' was, in fact, nothing but a simple *yoga* exercise and if you thought that you had seen the image of a Brahmanical punishment for the death of the holy cow, it might just have been that the poor man had let the cow die because the Brahmin couldn't give him enough to feed either himself or his cow.

We moved slowly along the *ghats* towards the south. An enormous man, who reminded me of Ram Lal, the telephone-wala in Allahabad, hurriedly undressed, revealing a hairy and chubby body, enough to make a pig jealous. Feeling the steps with his feet, he entered the waters till Ganga reached his waist. There, he stood silent, eyes closed, hands folded before the sun, and murmured a short prayer. Then, bowing his head, he took a handful of the sacred waters and offered them, bit by bit, to the east, to the south, to the west, to the north, wherever the universe existed. Then, suddenly, with electric swiftness, he shoved his hand into his underwear and began to vigorously scrub the sins of his phallus and rectum. Seeing him perform the frantic ritual, the lady next to him hastily turned her eyes the other way. At the other end, the view was no less comical. A Brahmin was washing his *janeou*, the sacred white thread that ran across his torso, like a sling. Holding the *janeou* tightly in his fist, and washing it at the waist level, his furious back and forth movements would easily have won him Salvador Dali's prize for the 'grand masturbator...'

We rowed down further, towards the Tulsidas *ghat*, where the poet-saint is said to have translated the *Ramayana* into Hindi. Along the wall behind the *ghat*, six young men sat on their haunches, pants pulled down to knees, shirts tied in a bow-knot at the waist, and a *beedi* in the mouth. Between each pair of legs dropped a scoop of 'grey matter', enveloped in white steam to remind us that the distinguished gentlemen were defecating before the wintry witness of the holy river. Soon, six streams of urine cascaded down the holy *ghat* to merge their destiny with the immortal waters of Goddess Ganga. With the two waters thus united, the human and the heavenly, Om asked me:

'Do you mind if we have a quick dip here? To bathe at this *ghat* is extremely auspicious.' Within minutes, Om and Jagdish could be seen swimming like swans.

Since we had left Allahabad two days ago, this was the first time that I found myself alone on the boat. In the midst of tens of thousands of pilgrims, I felt helplessly alone, my body trembled.

That Jaya was to arrive later in the evening, that I was condemned to relive the pain of a love which I had still not overcome, enkindled in me the cowardly desire to flee Benares. I left the boat and stepped out on to the *ghat*. Millions of pilgrims and vendors surrounded me, but my vision registered nothing. In a city where Ganga offered calm to everyone, it seemed that the holy goddess had singled me out for the most agonizing solitary imprisonment. Sweating, trembling, I was walking down towards the bridge when someone thumped me hard on my back and exclaimed: 'Incredible! Unbelievable! I didn't expect to meet you here, Nishant.' Just when I needed someone by my side the most, I found Claude, one of my closest friends from Paris, who had also known Jaya.

'So how are you? How is your Ganga going?' he asked, referring to my journey down Ganga. 'You look so haggard!'

'Yes. A bit shaken today.'

'Why?'

'Oh! Just that...'

'Don't tell me you've fallen in love again!'

'No.'

'What happened? You're not looking your normal self.'

'She's coming.'

'Who?'

'Jaya.'

'What? Again!'

'Yes. I got this mysterious telegram in Allahabad that she'll meet me here today at the hour of sunset. Strange...?'

'Where's she coming from?'

'No idea.'

'Was she in India?'

'I don't know. The telegram came from Delhi.'

'So she's in Delhi.'

'Presumably.'

'Do you think she has divorced her husband?'

'Not a clue.'

'Strange! I thought it had all ended in Paris. What a woman! She can't live without springing surprises every other day.'

'And you? What has brought you here?'

'Nothing special. In Paris, the weather was horrible, minus

ten. I couldn't take it. So I left for a holiday. But, tell me, when did she say she was coming?'

'This evening, at the hour of sunset!'

'Sounds so very Shakespearean! Anyway, come, let's go for a stroll down the *ghats*. I love this city.' As we walked down the *ghats* towards the overbridge, Claude remarked: 'It's incredible, this city! I've met three friends from Paris in the past twenty-four hours. These *ghats* are like the Boulevard St. Germain. You're walking down and, suddenly, you meet an old acquaintance. Have a drink with him, revive a friendship and, then, again you meet another... Long live the banks of Ganga.'

We had been on the *ghats* for barely ten minutes when a graceful, middle-aged gentleman, dressed in a white *kurta-pyjama* and a black waistcoat, walked up to me and greeted me. It was Shameem, Zehra's father. It must have been absent-mindedness, if not outright indifference, on my part that I asked him: 'What are you doing here!' Zehra's Hindu mother had died, and Shameem was on the *ghats* to immerse the ashes of his *tawaiff*-wife. That Zehra and Shabnam had not accompanied him to Benares was understandable because, in Hinduism, women do not participate in funeral rites. Gazing at the majestic flow of Ganga, Shameem said, in his poetic manner. 'All life must end here, Nishant *bhai*. Kings, queens, beggars, criminals, politicians, they all find their last home in these waves. And look at her, serene, unmindful, least concerned by the pain of her million pilgrims...' I placed my hand on Shameem's shoulder, 'Come, come, *honsla rakhiye*, this is life', and we walked down to a small restaurant near the Vishwanath Temple. Shameem, conscious of the foreigner in our company, asked Claude:

'This is your first time in Benares?'

'No, fifth.'

'Allah! You must be in love with the city, then!'

'I am, it's so beautiful!' said Claude, little realizing that Shameem was here to complete the funeral rites of his wife. 'I love the *ghats*, the sunrise, these parasols, the whole place. There's such purity about this place. We've lost this in the west.'

'Where are you from?'

'Paris.'

'Oh! Great city. City of Rimbaud and Baudelaire...'

'You know them?'

'Yes. Great masters.'

'He's a well-known poet himself,' I informed Claude.

'I love your religion,' Claude said to Shameem, sipping tea. 'I don't think I know of another city with such harmony.'

'Well, if you say so, you must be right. I personally don't believe in religion, neither Hinduism nor Islam. My wife had wished that her ashes be immersed in Ganga, so I've come here...'

'I'm sorry to hear that,' said Claude, apologetically, realising his *faux pas*.

'This is life. Wounds of death can only heal with time.' remarked Shameem, philosophically, 'but your earlier statement sounds interesting. Do you really think that Benares looks pure?'

'Yes.'

'Don't you think this purity is a mask? Purity is actually a search of the self–in fact, that what results from an honest search of ourselves. What you see in Benares is not that!'

'Yes, I see what you mean. But these sunrises in Benares look so pure.'

'Yes, but these sunrises are very different from the path of truth. Do you know, very few pilgrims follow the path of life that they may be chanting on their lips? Belief, meditation, thought, they imply a deep search of the self.'

'I agree.'

'I'm sorry to be saying this to you, especially when you're

a visitor to our country. But I feel the need to tell the truth. When I was on Ganga this morning, I hated this spectacle of hypocrisy. None of these pilgrims have given up their pleasures or vices. They are unscrupulous. They make money through the worst possible means. They're full of hatred, suspicion, dishonesty. And when they come to Benares, they float a few lamps, and they think their sins are forgiven. In fact, they need this theatre precisely because they know they are guilty.'

'But look at the river!' persisted Claude in his defence of Benares. 'It looks so beautiful and calm.'

'What calmness! Do you know these very pilgrims on the banks of Ganga could suddenly become the worst butchers in history?' Shameem turned towards me and asked: 'What do you say, Nishant bhai?'

'I agree. Someone once said that the waters of Ganga irrigate the fields of Hindu-Muslim communalism!'

'Precisely!' agreed Shameem, whose wife had been the victim of a Hindu-Muslim riot. Infuriated with the world of fanatic beliefs, Shameem said aloud: 'This harmonious sunrise of Benares, Claude *bhai*, is an illusion. A Muslim finds his pig maltreated, he slaughters his Hindu neighbour. A Hindu sees his cow beaten by a Muslim, he unleashes terror on the Muslims in his city...'

Overhearing our animated conversation, the muscular, oily-skinned restaurant owner, with the sacred Brahmanical thread proudly cutting across his torso, swaggered up to Shameem and said threateningly:

'*Arre Mian*, if you need to give these long Islamic lectures to young, innocent minds, find yourself another restaurant. So long as we live, this holy city will be safe in the hands of the Hindus. And don't you dare come to this restaurant again! It belongs to the Hindu Mahasabha.'

Sunset

SUNSET

Jaya

JAYA CAME. SHE LEFT. IT IS TO TELL THIS TRUTH THAT I began writing this book. I am guilty. I do not know the truth. And what I do not know, I cannot tell. I plead guilty. I have made you travel long into the face of a shameful disappointment. Jaya came. She left. That alone is the truth.

There is a point in consciousness where nothing exists. Shock. Emptiness. Silence. Void. Trance. Hollow. Vacuity, Vacuum. So many words and, yet, nothing captures the essence of this point, the point of life, the point of death, the point of Jaya. It is to discover this point that Benares raised itself through the ages. And if Benares *is*, it is not because its *yogis* found this point, but precisely because it was never found.

There is a moment in life when the spirit abandons the body and, they say, it is still alive. Life becomes the miraculous product of a biological caprice. You live not because you live, but because something else lives within you. Cells. Blood. Genes. An entire metabolism that life has nothing to do with, and yet, that alone is life.

The heart beats for the world has ceased to beat anymore.

Dregs

'But I still like you.'
'I have loved you.'
'I have wept for you.'
'I don't know how it happened
'Believe me, it was beyond me.'
'I couldn't help it.'
'Say something.'
'I beg of you, say something.'
'Your silence worries me.'
'Your sorrow benumbs me.'
'Say something.'
'Just one word, Nishant.'
'But I still like you.'
'We are still friends.'
'We'll be friends forever.'
Friendship, I spit in your face.

Clochard

I WAS IN A NARROW ALLEY BEHIND THE VISHWANATH temple. Suddenly, I felt the urge to cry. To weep. Frenzied crowds surrounded me. How to cry! Where? I didn't want to shed tears in public, before the holy city saw in my sorrow the sorrow of its own birth. I rushed into a tiny street, sat on a doorstep and wept bitterly. Seeing me hysterical, a dog came from the back and barked: 'Get up! Hey, you tramp, get up! *Quel clochard d'amour!*'

Nothingness

'then even nothingness was not, nor existence.
there was no air, nor the heavens beyond it.
who covered it? where was it? in whose keeping?
was there then cosmic water, in depths unfathomed…?
but, after all, who knows, and who can say,
whence it all came, and how creation happened?
the gods themselves are later than creation,
so who knows truly whence it has arisen?'

Tell me, Ganga, where disappeared Jaya
And where appeared you.

Grammar

L OVE IS, HAD SAID JAYA.
Love *was*, said Jaya now.

The game of tenses. Present. Simple past. How incredibly simple... Benares taught me the basic elements of the grammar of love.

I felt displaced. Someone had conquered my *id*, the point where rises desire, where dies desire, where it swells, where it faints. In the secret space of my mind, I saw Jaya with a German. I was told the gentleman smoked a pipe, he read *Der Speigel*. He liked water, beaches, children, he was sportive. His English was rusty, so he mistook monks for monkeys but, still, he was a cultured man. He had eyes like mine, he had a lovely voice and he introduced himself as Wolfgang Müller.

Love is the domain of freedom. Everyone has the right to free choice. You pick one, you drop the other. She has the liberty, the moral right, even a constitutional right. But her right to her freedom is the theft of my freedom. She stole from me, and gave to another what she had given me, and that which had already become mine. Born blind, she gave me the eyes to witness, that blindness was better than the sordid landscape of these vampires of love.

Attente

आहिस्ता आहिस्ता मेरा हिन्दुस्तान खिसक रहा था और मैं धीरे धीरे देख रहा था गायबानी का तमाशा। और मैं देख रहा था रफ्ता रफ्ता अज़ीयों के साथ साथ धीमें धीमें टूटना दम तोड़ना आकांक्षाओं के इक समूह का। ऊपरों से गिरते पड़ते थे उम्मीद के दीवारों दर। ढलते ढलते ढल रही थी पेंगू की विरासत। और अंत के कालीन में छुप रहा था जो भी था।

फिर अक्सर मैंने देखा दूर से आते हुए इक आशाना रूमाल को। जाना पहचाना मेरा हम साया हम नवाज़ सा। अक्सर हिया करता हुआ, हँसता हुआ, गाता हुआ। हिंद के तुग़लिए का नाज़ुक तन डोलता ठहरने लगा मेरी तरफ़। और मैं अनजान बन दूसरी तरफ़ देखने लगा। और पूछता फिरता रहा इस वक़्त का क्या नाम है। क्या नाम है इस वक़्त का?

ठंडा के मुझको इल्म है कि जीस्त इक व्यवस्था है। और इस वक़्त का कोई नाम नहीं।

I liked the prose. It spoke of an identical destiny. This unknown poet and I seemed to have taken the same boat down Ganga. The only difference: he didn't seek anything of Ganga, and I perhaps did. Ganga betrays when you need her the most...

Beach

I strolled away from Benares along Ganga inwards, into proximity to the self. There, I discovered a beach which had the eye-lashes of kaya and the colors of her purple breasts. I scribbled on the sand of treacherous times.

Dear Lay,
I thought of writing to you. I don't know why. Sorrow, void, surprise, convulsion... in all this, I'm drove you to have a place somewhere. Is that you on the breast of sand hay someone lying back, waiting for the night to crawl over the circularity of time, that the icicet of lies has not touched the warmth of our grilled childhood is yet another proof of friendships that shall bloom in graveyard alone. I wish you love and happiness. Nishad.

Beauty?
Spark of real with dream.

Pain?
Necessity.

Guilt?
debt of humanity to morality, recoverable in pints of blood.

Memory and desire meet at cross-roads. Each looks at the other, they pass, without exchanging a word.

BEACH 183

Love?
walls of shadows
in the houses of
Photo...

I have dug graves, and have often
found in them corpses alive and
palpitating. All my loves had one
common corpse. It was pale
green, the colour of spring.

Objective Chance?
Clean white bed
sheets... and the
earring she'd
forgotten, aflame...

Scream?
A beach where I am
the lone promenader
and my shadow,
my lover.

to paris
on lips forgotten
on lips retouched
on the clock of surprises
i write your name...
    Oui, c'est moi, Eluard!
    A ta santé, Paul!

Jaya,
Murder in the
mirror of
Suicide... alas!

Politics?
Praying mid-dreams for
peaceful death of all humans
in a single womb.

Real?
Flesh becoming tortoise-shell.

अलविदा..

As I was scribbling, a fish popped out of water and
landed on the sand. It tossed, turned, wriggled,
quivered. Then calm, she lay dead. I put her
back into Ganga. Laughing, she said, "may all
brides be Benares born..."

Revolt

A WHOLE DECADE AFTER READING IT FIRST, I understood what André Breton had meant by this passage from the Second Manifesto of Surrealism:

'The simplest surrealist act consists in dashing down the street, pistol in hand, and firing blindly, as fast as you can pull the trigger, into the crowd. Anyone who, at least once in his life, has not dreamt of thus putting an end to the petty system of debasement and cretinisation in effect has a well-defined place in that crowd, with his belly before the barrel.'

Theft

IT FEELS AS THOUGH I'VE BEEN ROBBED. NOT OF MY SOUL. Nor of life. Nor of sentiment. Nothing as abstract as that. Something very real that a lover alone can steal in life.

Yes, I know what she stole. She stole a violet ribbon from my stomach. By mistake, I had left the edge of the ribbon exposed at my navel. The thief found it. Then, she pulled at it. Metres and metres of it, kilometres and kilometres of it, wrinkled, knotted, tangled, she pulled at it for weeks without pause or respite. Till the ribbon ended, held by a tiny knot on the navel.

The ribbon lay before me. Violet, stretches and stretches of it, fluttering in the icy wind. I could see life outside myself, my own life outside its own cocoon. Inside, there was nothing. It was all empty, exhausted, finished. I could neither live nor die.

Jaya, she was a thief.

Krishna

MY GANGA REFUSED TO FLOW ANY MORE. FOR SEVERAL days after Jaya left, I lived on the *ghats*. I spent my time sitting, musing, staring into meaningless distances. One day, far from Benares, I was sitting on the sandy shores of the river. Lost, puzzled, I had had enough of this unending life. An old man, a *sadhu* who didn't resemble a *sadhu*, walked up to me, smiled kindly and said, 'You are sad.' I did not answer. He came closer, and repeated: 'You're sad, aren't you?' I noticed that he had a deep and pleasant voice. His big but soft build, broad features, long flowing hair, and thick, drooping lips emanated human warmth, but I was not in a state of mind to speak of things which had little meaning in life. As I looked away, he spoke again:

'You're sad, aren't you? Tell me, my son, are you sad?'

'Yes.'

'Why are you sad?'

'If I knew, I wouldn't be sad. Please leave me alone, *baba*. I want to be alone.'

'You're sad because of attachment?'

'Yes.'

'Your wife left you.'

'I am not married.'

'Your *premi* left you. Someone you loved has caused you pain.'

'Yes. But I beg of you, *baba*, I want to be alone.'

'I will leave you alone. I cannot but leave you alone. But I've been sent to help you.'

'What!'

'Yes, I've been sent to help you.' said *baba*, with the authority of a father. Placing his cloth-bag on the ground, he said commandingly:

'Come, stand up and hold a coin in your hand.'

The Socratic air around him had by now begun to disarm me. Standing up on my feet, I asked him:

'Coin? What do you mean?'

'Any coin. Take a coin from your pocket and hold it in your fist.' I took a ten paisa coin and placed it on my palm. 'Fold your fist, and hold it tight,' he ordered. Withdrawing three metres away, with one finger pointed towards my fist, *baba* shut his eyes, and produced a whistling sound from his mouth. Within minutes, the coin in my hand started to heat up. Seconds later, it became burning hot. I clenched my fist harder to fight back the burning. The hand burnt faster. I let the fist loose, and the coin dropped. I looked at my hand. It was partly burnt, and the aluminium ash from the embossing on the coin had silver-greyed my sweating palm. Just as I was examining and re-examining my palm in disbelief, *baba* laughed lazily and said:

'You're sad, my son, aren't you?'

'Yes.'

'You had loved.'

'Like so many others.'

'Did she belong to the south of India?'

'She did.'

'Her name began with a 'J'?'

'Yes.'

Baba laughed with the confidence of a soothsayer.

'Was she born in the month of *Ashwin*?'

'Yes.'
'On the fifteenth?'
'Yes.'
'At five-fifteen in the morning?'
'I don't know.'
'But I know.'
'You seem to know everything.'
'Yes, I do.'
'But what happened, *baba*?'
'You betrayed her.'
'How?'
'By breaking your promise.'
'How?'
'By wanting to write this book. Hadn't you promised her something?'
'Yes.'
'But why are you sad?' asked *baba*, placing his heavy wrinkled hand on my shoulder.
'Because it is all over.'
'Had it ever begun?'
'No.'
'So? What is not born, how can it ever die?'
He told me a little story from the *Upanishads*.
'Fetch me a fruit from the banyan tree,' said the father.
'Here is one, sir.'
'Break it.'
'I have broken it, sir.'
'What do you see?'
'Very tiny seeds, sir.'
'Break one.'
'I have broken it.'
'What do you see now?'

'Nothing, sir.'

'My son.' said the father, 'what you do not perceive is the essence, and in that essence the mighty banyan tree exists. Believe me, my son, in that essence is the self of all that is. That is the truth, that is the self...'

His story perplexed me. There was little connection between his story and his earlier conversation. I asked him:

'But why did you tell me this story?'

'Because you are in search of your self.'

'Like so many others.'

'But you are about to abandon your search. Aren't you thinking of giving up your journey?'

'Which journey?'

'Hadn't you decided to go down Ganga?'

'Yes. How did you guess that?'

'Your boatmen told me.'

'You know them?'

'Yes.'

'What did they tell you?'

'That you were sad and about to abandon your journey.'

'So they told you about Jaya.'

'No, nothing.'

'Then how did you know about Jaya?'

'*Yogis* know. Intuition and other forms of knowledge come only to a true *yogi*. If you like, I can tell you more about yourself.'

'Have the boatmen left, *baba*?'

'They left this morning. I saw them leave.'

'*Baba*, have you ever been sad?'

'Who hasn't! I was like any other man on this earth.'

'What is sorrow?'

'Five vices–Anger, attachment, sexual desire, greed, intoxication.'

'Did you never have them?'

'I had them all. I was like any other human being. I was married to a woman called Radhika. I knew that a woman was *Kamini*, the goddess of sexual desire, but I also knew that only by living with lust could you overcome lust. After a few years, I left home. I did all kinds of jobs. I was a car mechanic, a forest guard, even a policeman for six months. One day, a *guru* asked me to become a *yogi*. Over the years, I learnt the path to attain the supreme being. Now I do not know any sorrow.'

'But why do you want me to continue my journey down Ganga, baba?'

'You must not abandon your search.'

'I do not feel like pursuing it.'

'Because you have accepted defeat.'

'Perhaps.'

'Why?'

'Because I am sad and mortal. I just want to find an obscure corner of this world and write. I find solace in writing.'

'But Gangaji is a poem.'

'So you think.'

'So you thought, didn't you?'

'Yes, but no longer. I have lost faith in her.'

'These are mere excuses, my son. The fact is that you have let yourself overcome by the earthly.'

'Perhaps.'

Disappointed in me, *baba* picked up his cloth-bag, and walked away as mysteriously as he had arrived.

Swells

THE AFTERMATH OF LOVE RESEMBLES THE BOILS OF MILK. I am a pot of milk, placed on a constant flame. I swell up towards the brim. Then, someone like *baba* removes me from the heat. I unswell. I calm down, and rediscover my bearings in life. I go back to the heat, for the flame is my fate, my home. Suddenly, I swell up again. I cry out in anguish: 'Help, help, I'm about to boil over.' Baba appears again. I unswell. The cycle carries on. This is life.

The words of the *yogi* must have comforted me, because I recommenced my journey that morning. Ganga looked beautiful again, like a bride wrapped up in a million colours. We crossed the railway bridge on our way to Ghazipur. To our left, the famous burning *ghats* of Benares were busy delivering people to the heavens. The sunrise, the birds, the dolphins, the green slopes, Ganga and her immortal family, had returned to guide me through the pains of human love. It is precisely after moments of pain that the world appears beautiful again.

By now, I had learnt the art of rowing. My movements synchronised with those of the new boatmen, and with six oars to a boat the flow was indeed perfect. The morning mist had just about dissolved when our boat approached a dead body. The boatman asked me to stop rowing and to hold the oars up in the air. I obeyed. The boat slowed down as it neared the corpse. Hari Ram, the navigator sitting up in front, looked at the body closely, and muttered: 'It hasn't even been covered. Seems as if the woman committed suicide.' The body, its front facing upwards, floated lazily towards me. It was young, sensual, beautiful. Suddenly I felt the milk swell up in my head, and unconsciously, I picked up an oar and slammed it hard on the head of the body. The boatmen went mad, as I already had.

'Haven't you ever lost someone in your family!'

'You have no respect for the human soul, you heartless foreigner.'

'Cruel hearted!'

'Murderer!'

'Don't you have a sister?'

'Don't you have a mother?'

But I loved her, bhaiya...

'Shameless bastard! You do this to a young woman's body, and you have the audacity to say you love women!'

'Pain! Haven't you ever felt pain!'

'I could beat you to pulp!'

'The villagers would have burnt you alive!'

'But, listen, bhaiya, I had loved, I had loved sincerely.'

'Is this what you call your love?'

'Men like you provoke suicides.'

'Get out of this boat!'

'I don't want to see you alive.'

'Throw him into the river!'

'You don't deserve to live!'

'Bastard!'

'Shameless!'

'Chandal!'

'Blood-sucker!'

'You have no right to live!'

'Yes, you're right, I have no right to live. Why didn't my mother

drown me right there and then when she first brought me to the banks of Benares? Why didn't she throttle me then? Why? Why'

'This chap's lost his head!'

'He's mad!'

'You should go to the mental asylum.'

'Hand him over to the police.'

'Go and see a doctor and have your brains fixed!'

Their anger could have killed me, they could have cut me to pieces, but they were kind and merciful. They took the boat to the far bank and cursing one last time, 'May you be eaten up by worms,' they left me in the middle of nowhere and rowed back towards Benares. Suddenly, a strange fright gripped me, I was petrified. I was afraid of being murdered and yet not dying; I was afraid of murdering, and yet not killing. All I can recollect is streams and streams of sweat running down my body.

Murder is the mirror of suicide, Jaya...

Fable

WHEN I WAS A CHILD, MY MOTHER WOULD COME AND sit by my jute-cot every night. Making me sip milk from a *kansi* glass, she would tell me stories about the world. There were gods, there were goddesses, there were fairies, there were nymphs, there was the sky, the earth, the nether-world. There was everything in them to tell the child that life unfolding before him was indeed beautiful. Childhood is far, very far, even too distant to recall the feel of those lovely cradles. Little has survived from those days, not even the voice that related those stories, but two things still live in my memory. First, her stories always had happy endings. The king found his queen, the *devas* defeated the *asuras*, Ganga rescued humanity and the beggar found a bag of gold. And, then, her stories were simple, incredibly simple. From a whole mesh of confusing battles and events, the story emerged like a clear skyline which could not but leave a lasting impression on the mind. I don't know why, after so long, I thought of the childhood stories. Perhaps because sorrow compels one to seek refuge in the mother and childhood, or because I felt that the rest of my story too was quite simple. Weeks after the incident with the Benares boatmen, my boat, rowed by another set of Bengali *majhis*, approached Calcutta. At first, I did not want to leave the boat, for a traveller on water is little different from a fish in water. Life on sea or on river, as on earth, is a universe complete in itself, with its own precise measure of time and space;

and just as an ordinary man cannot for long stand the pressures of the water-world, the man used being on water finds the earth too restrictive and active for his soul. And then, tragedies live differently on water. Water is a great healer. The constant flow of a boat, its monotonous rhythm, the plopping sound of fish and oars, are an innate antidote to the chagrin of human life. As I rowed deeper and deeper into Calcutta, the pandemonium of the city became increasingly unbearable. The head felt like an echo-chamber and horns, cries, shrieks, creakings, even laughter, each sound from the city made me flee towards the river. I asked the boatmen if they could row me a few kilometres beyond Calcutta. 'No, *dada*. We can't,' replied Swapan crisply 'it's soon going to be high-tide. This boat won't be able to take the force of water. At best, we can drop you at the harbour.'

I settled the account with the boatmen, picked up my bag, and walked out of a cluster of dilapidated constructions which once went by the name of the Imperial Calcutta Harbour. I waited for a taxi for over an hour, and when, finally, one did agree to take me, we ran into a demonstration. Seeing me restless, the driver tried to cool my nerves, and exhibiting a rare skill at handling the Calcutta crowd, he blew his horn, turned, twisted and squeezed in an effort to cut across the demonstration.

He managed to force his way up to a certain point, but by the time we reached the Calcutta Telephones building, which was also the dead centre of the demonstration, the taxi was hopelessly stuck and the driver, visibly upset, switched off the engine. Looking at the crowd, he muttered to himself: 'This is not a demonstration. It's a cremation.' Indeed, as I noticed myself, it was a cremation. To our right, a group of priests dressed in spotless white stood on the steps of the Telephone building, busy preparing the funeral rites. The sight of a cremation in the heart of Calcutta perplexed me. I asked the driver:

'Any idea who has died?'

'Don't know. Must be someone.'

'Strange! A cremation in a government office! Isn't it prohibited by law?'

'Who told you, *babu*, that there was law in Bengal!' remarked the driver, with bitter sarcasm.

'Why do you say that?'

'Because law disappeared with the Congress rule in Bengal. The Communists have only brought in lawlessness. Look at this! A cremation right behind the Writers' building! If our Congress had been in power, the Chief Minister would have had them shot!'

With little chance of getting out of the funeral procession in a taxi, I left the Congress-sympathizer to himself, tipping him an extra tenner to cool his temper. Picking up my bag, I started to cut across the crowd. The mystery around the cremation, however, deepened as the priests lit the funeral pyre and soon, two-metre-high flames were fluttering in the wind, surrounded by the loud chanting of a funeral hymn. Still puzzled by this cremation, I walked up to a mourner and asked him politely:

'Pardon my ignorance, *dada*, but who has died?'

'You don't even know that?' He was astonished.

'I am sorry I don't.'

'Funny, you're in a procession and you don't even know what for!'

'Sorry, I am not in the procession.'

'Then you had better be,' he said laughing, 'well, you see the people of Calcutta have come to cremate the bogus, hopeless, third-rate, good-for-nothing telephones of this city. This was the only means left for protesting against our telephones which pass for the ultra-modern and space-age technology of India...'

The crowd relished each adjective defining the Indian telephones with peals of laughter, but I was not quite in the frame of mind to enjoy their company for long. It must have been around noon. Calcutta was getting sultrier with the sun. I walked down to Park Lane and picked up some lunch. As I was walking out of the restaurant, someone thumped me hard on the back and screamed:

'*Dis-donc, c'est toi!* Good heavens, is that you?'

'Oh! *Bonjour. Ca va?* I replied hesitantly, not quite able to place the man on the spur of the moment.

'You don't recall me?' he said, winking at the charming Indian girl by his side.

His typical manner of winking, and the sly smile that went with it, gave the secret away, and I knew that the man facing me was Patrick Chalandon, a seasoned French wheeler-dealer who had been in Calcutta for donkey's years. We had met some years ago at one of the semi-diplomatic parties of the Alliance Française, and I recollected that Patrick had, that evening, struck me as a smooth and unscrupulous man. If there was anything enviable about the man, it was his rare gift of superficiality. Bank accounts, scotch, women and boasting, summed up his mission in life. He felt human attachment was a trap and without a hint of embarrassment on his face, declared publicly that he could happily be making love to a woman one night and yet be thinking about the pending telephone and electricity bills he had to clear the next morning. Money was his god.

Sounding unbelievably friendly, Patrick insisted that I accompany him home. I refused. Looking slightly intrigued by my stubborn refusal, he asked:

'Do you have any appointments?'

'What appointments could I have with this bag on my shoulder?'

'So where's the problem? Come.'

'No thanks.'

'Where are you staying?'

'Nowhere as yet.'

'So...'

Patrick snatched my bag, the way long-lost friends do, and dumped it in his car. I gave in, for another refusal would have meant too much effort. And then, at a moment when I desired to be anonymous, Patrick was the ideal company for a frivolous drink. He did not know my past, he hadn't heard of my Ganga, he wouldn't raise the subject of my Zehras and Jayas. He was perfectly suited to kill time.

His bungalow on Lee Road spoke volumes for the wealth Patrick had amassed during his years in India. Antique sculptures, paintings, cut-glass, rose-wood furniture, *durbans*, he had everything to seduce a young, westernized Bengali spinster or a fawning business customer. Pouring me a glass of beer, he asked:

'So how's Mitterand doing? Good ole Francois? He's in trouble, isn't he?'

'There are ups and downs in everyone's career.'

'And what about the Sikhs boys? They blew up a plane!'

'Which plane?'

'It was near Paris, wasn't it?'

'No, you're thinking of the Air India plane. That was off the Irish coast.'

'Really?' asked Patrick, embarrassed, 'Don't know why I thought it was in the French air space. Anyway, how does it matter? There are things blowing up all over the place every day. Tell me, how's French football doing?'

'This is going to be Platini's last World Cup.'

'Did you know Satyajit Ray lives right round the corner?'

I noticed that Patrick was changing topics at an incredibly nervous pace. 'Yes, I know. Met him there once.'

'And there's this other chap doing an Indo-French film. That dark fellow with glasses.'

'You mean Mrinal Sen?'

'Probably. Oh! These Bengali names are *compliqués*. And how's Paris?'

'Aren't you planning to go back?'

'Me? Never. Once you're used to the chaos of Calcutta, you can't live anywhere else. Oh no! Paris for me is past. Like my first wife.' Patrick got up, served me some more beer, and then, inspecting my face closely, he remarked:

'Look at you! You look like a tramp!'

'Yes, I am a bit tired.'

'Did you have to wait long at the airport?'

'I came by train.'

'Why not, why not!' said Patrick. 'Train journeys can be great fun. But only if you have the time for them. Indian trains are so painfully slow. Tell me, how's the TGV doing in France?'

Patrick's tirade of meaningless questions was beginning to get on my nerves and for a moment I thought he had invited me home purely because he had no one better to talk to. Reversing the tide of interrogation, I asked him:

'And what about you? Bank accounts, money, women, are they still your only goal in life? I see you still fancy pretty women.'

'Oh! You mean the girl who was with me... She's not bad really. Perhaps a shade too Bengali for my taste though. Indian women get attached so quickly. Quite silly!'

'Still selling your *objets d'art*?'

'I gave that up ages ago. Oh no! I wasn't going to waste my life on idols and ivory lamps. I am into bigger things now. Into trains.'

'Trains?'

'Yes, yes. You'll see, one of these days we might bag a contract worth 4000 million rupees.' Patrick lit a *Habana* cigar.

'You've started consultancy services, have you?'

'In a way. One day I thought, why do these petty deals and contracts? So much sweat and such little money. So I got into something that India needed badly.'

'But India has one of the largest rail networks in the world.'

'Exactly. And look at the way it functions! Do you know what the average speed of a train in India is? Twenty-five kilometres an hour! The trains here are snails on wheels. So I thought why not revolutionise the railways in India, and try and get the TGV in.'

'You're going to sell coaches to India, is it?'

'Coaches and other things—electric locomotives, tracks, signalling equipment, everything. We need to get the trains moving in India... I have brought a French company into this. We might clinch the deal you know. *Insha Allah!*'

'So Monsieur Chalandon is going to be the man behind the next Bofors scandal!'

'Bofors! Bullshit!' fumed Patrick, 'The Indian press is stupid! What's wrong with the Bofors deal? Everyone pays kickbacks for work done. It's accepted practice in the trade. Oh! Indians are paranoid... But hang on a minute. Let me just check if there was any mail this morning. I am expecting an important letter from Delhi.'

Gopuda, Patrick's servant, walked in with four letters and an ivory letter-opener placed on a silver tray, and literally offered them to his master, as if he were serving some dry fruit. Patrick went through most of the mail very quickly but, I noticed, that he read the last letter twice. Putting the letter back in the envelope, he said grimly:

'That's sad!'

'What happened?' I tried to show concern.

'Very sad!'

'There are ups and downs in business.'

'No, no.' said Patrick, a bit impatiently, 'It has nothing to do with business. Something personal. A French friend has lost his wife. He sounds shattered in this letter.'

'Sorry to hear that.'

'Oh! Haven't I always said human attachments are a trap. Anyway, she's dead, she's dead, what can be done? But what a silly way of dying!'

'What happened?'

'Got swept away by the waves. The sea is treacherous.'

'Was she young?'

'Twenty-five odd. Beautiful girl. A real beauty. I knew her in Calcutta. In fact, I had a massive crush on her. Anyway, gone is gone. Her husband is in a bad shape.'

'But what was she doing in the sea in a European winter? It's very cold in France this winter.'

'Did I say she was in Europe?'

'No, but I thought so.'

'She was in Pakistan. An Indian married to a French teacher.'

'In Pakistan?'

'Yes, in Karachi.'

'What was her name?'

'I don't think you could have known her. She was called Jaya.'

'Oh! Jaya.'

'You knew her, did you?'

I left his house and wandered about the streets of Calcutta all night. I suddenly felt free, madly free. There were no liabilities, no accounts to settle with life, nothing to take, nothing to give. I just felt free, dementedly free...

Funeral

THE POT WAS EMPTY. THE MILK HAD COMPLETELY boiled over. Only the flame was still lit, flickering, free, like Ganga, like Jaya.

She loved the waters. They were her passion, her poetry, her gamble, the test of her strength. Jaya did not take on small dangers. Proud and arrogant, she threw her arms open only to the worst risks that life had ever known. She loved turbulence, turbulence of the worst waters, turbulence of the men who she knew would entangle her life inextricably. My greatest dream, she had said once, is to dance like a dolphin in the seas. It was not an accident, then, that her smile was borrowed from the waves of the Mediterranean, and her complexion from the sky. Only swimmers deserve to drown, they say. From the seas she had come and to the seas she had now returned, summoned by the orders of an unpredictable destiny.

God is a fool. He could not have been more stupid. The blank pages of Benares, the death of Zehra's mother at the hands of a Hindu fascist, Jaya's suicide in Karachi... I could laugh at this necklace of tragedies. God is a fool, as death is a farce. God does not realise that he must torture man only to a point where his spirit does not die. Once dead, the man dies and so does God. The fool does not understand that he is, because man is, and if he negates man, he negates himself. Death itself is dead. Where is death? Not in Jaya, nor in Smita. Jaya lives just as

Smita lives, but only death is dead and as for God, the less said the better, he is simply a fool.

Absolved, unchained, freed at last, I reached the midnight funeral convened at the very feet of Ganga called the Gangasagar. The flames rose high, their tips touched the moon. Waves secreted silver, the ocean turned into a mine. Waves and waves of molten silver rolled away into a horizon of unfulfilled desires. The boat was turbulent. The wind had lost her balance. The waves rose high, we higher, and the flames, yet higher. Hey wind, have you gone mad? Have you lost the melody in your flute? And Ganga, you? Have you gone mad, too? Have you lost the calm that renders you divine? Come Ganga, tell me the end of my story. Do you promise me the same fate that you condemned your husband, Shantanu, to? Hey Ganga, do you know the ocean is mounting up to your breast? Hey moon, do you still think you are invincible?

Moon, hey full-moon, don't be arrogant, for you know that you find your birth-cry in my eye. You are too proud moon. I condemn you. You will carry forever the scar of my guilt on your face. And remember, you arrogant moon, that on the day of Judgement, you shall face my trial. Remember, trials there were many, but Kafka there was one.

> And you, waves,
> you capricious waves
> you smile you play
> you seduce you play
> come,
> show me Jaya
> show me light
> show me my love
> you hide behind your veil.

Hey, Jaya
Jaya
can you hear me, Jaya?
open the door
it's midnight
don't be scared
it's not a thief
it's not a criminal
it's me, Jaya.

Hey, Jaya,
open the door
are you asleep
fast asleep?
hey, Jaya, wake up,
i've run away from the jail
the guards were asleep
the sentinels were drunk
wake up, Jaya,
the cops are on my trail.

Hey, Jaya,
come, wake up,
betray the gods
sneak through the cover of waves
wake up, Jaya.
i know you are shy
but there's no one around
the boatmen have gone
bhanu, the little boy,
is asleep
rise, Jaya, rise.

You said,
my words rhythm your silences
here,
i offer you the poem of our creation
and our end.

come rise,
rise from the forest of photons
slip through the bracelet of waves
come, raise your liquid veil
and wear your silver ring.

Java,
come, wake up.
look, it's begun to rain
the mercurial rain
the fluorescent rain
the beautiful rain
the rain that made Ganga
that made the sea
and me, and you,
and all we had ever loved.

'I'll never be friends with the rain again,' were her last words.

Acknowledgements

I had never met him. I had never seen him. I had never read him. He was only a voice to me - a telephone voice that came into my life days before the outbreak of the Coronavirus pandemic. But this was also the voice I exchanged with for hours and hours over 2020, and we spoke of virtually everything under the sun—love, life, death, poetry, music, rivers, mountains...

This voice belonged to Mangalesh Dabral, the wonderful Hindi poet who is no more today. Sadly, he will forever remain a voice to me. Farewell, Mangalesh, please accept my sincerest gratitude for the care and kindness of both head and heart with which you translated this book into Hindi. It was a privilege to work with you, and to relive and recreate in another language, through laughter and bonhomie and Covid fears, the words and images of this book's journey. I had always said to you that the words of your own poetry reminded me of the lightness of a butterfly. How little did I know that this butterfly would flap away so soon forever, well before the publication of Jaya Ganga in Hindi and English. In your death, Coronavirus has cast its funeral shadow on the pages of this book.

As this work was first published nearly thirty-five years ago in English and French by Penguin Books and Editions Ramsay respectively, I would once again like to thank David Davidar, Toney Lacey, Paul Fournel, Khushwant Singh and Kapish Mehra for their generous investment in my loves and fantasies. Thanks to Amy Bhatt Potter and Meenakshi Suri, for accepting to ruin their respective holidays and reading through my manuscript; not only did they spent time over it, they even had the grace to say they actually enjoyed doing it.

Writing in many ways is an act of suicide. Each gesture of friendship helps in evading or accomplishing it. My thanks to Ann Ninan, Mukul Manglik, Harsh Kapoor, Lajpat Jagga, Yogesh Sharma, Burmi and Shailendra Mudgal for their support in running a household in Paris that was crumbling under the weight of meaningless deadlines and man-made paranoias. To Nandini Mehta for her unforgettable words of encouragement: She was the first person to read the manuscript way back in 1985.

To Usha Khurana, KP Singh, Tilak Raj Khorana, Sanjeev Ahluwalia, Paban Das Baul and Victoria Mukerji, for their boundless logistical and emotional support in making this difficult journey down the Ganga possible.

My thanks to Christine Cornet and the French Institute, Delhi, for their generous support towards the simultaneous publication of the English and Hindi editions of this book.

I feel too small to thank Elisa Breton, the wife of André Breton, the founder of surrealism, for the simple reason that there are certain artistic and moral debts in life that one can never pay off. Elisa's friendship and all the memory of André that came alive with it, is the most precious gift that this city of surrealists could have offered me.

But above all, it is to Mandakini, my love, yes, the very reincarnation of Ganga, to whom I repeat André Breton's words: 'I have discovered the secret of loving you, always for the first time.'

Paris, April 2021